HUNTSMAN

FOX HOLLOW ZODIAC NOVEL 1

MORGAN BRICE

ebook ISBN: 978-1-64795-005-7
Print ISBN: 978-1-64795-006-4

Cover art by Adrijus Guscia and Melissa Gilbert.
Darkwind Press is an imprint of DreamSpinner Communications, LLC

HUNTSMAN
A FOX HOLLOW ZODIAC NOVEL 1

By Morgan Brice

1

LIAM

JUST REMEMBERING THE HUNTSMAN MADE LIAM SHUDDER AND SENT HIS heart pounding.

He'd been lucky to get away. A Huntsman rarely made mistakes. Not when a prize like Liam was up for grabs. If a friend hadn't tipped him off, he would probably be dead by now—or worse. As it was, his escape had been too close.

Liam didn't own much—putting himself through graduate school to get his master's in library science didn't leave a lot extra for luxuries. His apartment had been furnished with thrift store bargains and trash-day cast-offs, but it was snug and comfortable. Then the call came from a friend, and Liam had just enough time to throw all his clothing into a duffel bag, grab some favorite photos and books, plus his two best pans, and pack his laptop, wallet, and phone before going out the window and down the fire escape.

Through the apartment's video feed, Liam had glimpsed the Huntsman picking the lock at the main front door. By being fast and silent—and barricading the door to his bedroom as a delaying tactic—Liam earned a few minutes leeway to get to his car before his would-be killer realized he was gone.

Being a fox shifter meant knowing how to be tricky. Of course, being a fox shifter was exactly what got him into trouble in the first place.

LIAM'S HANDS tightened around the steering wheel as he tried to get his breathing under control. He glanced into the backseat of his old Honda Civic, double-checking that his computer bag and duffel were there.

Spring came late to this part of Upstate New York, and temperatures could still drop below freezing, making for patches of black ice on the road. The last thing Liam needed now was to wreck. His ten-year-old car handled well on snow and started reliably in cold weather — qualities he'd need where he was going. Liam shivered in his light jacket. He owned a decent winter coat—which he had remembered to grab from his closet, along with his boots, gloves, scarf, and hat—since Ithaca still got plenty of snow. But winter in Fox Hollow, way up in the Adirondack Mountains, promised to be a whole new experience.

Screw it. I can deal with cold and snow. I can't deal with being hunted.

The warning call had come at six in the evening, not long after Liam had gotten home from his shift at the Ithaca College library, where he had landed an assistant librarian job after he finished his degree two years ago. The job he had just ditched, along with his apartment and friends, to run for his life.

Jeb was one of the few shifters Liam knew. So when Jeb's warning wasn't just that a hitman was after Liam, but a Huntsman—a legendary, near-mythical boogieman of a predator—Liam had dropped everything and fled.

He skidded, and for just a second, felt his tires lose traction. Liam eased off the gas pedal, steered into the skid, and evened out. If late spring was this cold and icy, he didn't want to think what real winter would hold.

Hyperventilating and passing out won't help.

Thank the gods for Dr. Jeffries. When his favorite undergrad professor left Ithaca for a new role at the Fox Institute, he told Liam that if he ever needed a job or a place to go in a pinch, to give him a call. Jeffries knew Liam didn't have any family to count on, and the two of them had bonded over a shared interest in mythology and folklore.

Just a few days ago, Jeffries had called to float a job opportunity by Liam—the head librarian position at the Fox Hollow Community Library, which also included managing the summer arts festival and the "Fall Fling" in conjunction with the Institute. At first glance, Liam had been perplexed, since while the role offered more creativity, it was also a step down in pay. He'd promised to think about it.

Then the warning came, and he ran. Now he needed a new job—far away from Ithaca.

Liam had called Jeffries from a rest stop a few hours ago to ask if the job was still open and if he could come up for an interview. Jeffries said that he'd taken the liberty of presenting Liam's resume to the search committee and that they wanted to offer Liam the job—which also included housing.

That's how things worked, Liam guessed, when your old prof taught at a place run by a bunch of psychics.

Liam had been gobsmacked, caught between feeling extremely grateful for a safe harbor and a little discombobulated over not actually having even interviewed. Jeffries had assured him they'd work everything out when he got there, and that he would explain it all. So Liam kept driving, but now he was running toward something instead of just away from the Huntsman.

He had his phone plugged into a cigarette-lighter adapter to play music and run his GPS, but the farther he got into the mountains, the more often the signal dropped. Once he was north of Utica, towns became fewer and farther between. Plenty of mountains, lakes, and forest filled in the gaps.

He had done a little research on his destination. Out of curiosity he had looked up Fox Hollow after Dr. Jeffries had called the first time. Fox Hollow had been partly settled by people from Lily Dale, a small community south of Buffalo founded by believers in the Spiritualist Movement—psychics, mediums, and those who believed that not only was there life after death, but that those with special talents could "pierce the Veil" and communicate with departed souls.

Liam had heard about three of the most famous Spiritualists, the

Fox Sisters. They gained fame in the late 1800s for their ability as mediums, only to fall into disgrace when one of them claimed their ability to speak with the dead was all a fraud. She recanted later, but the damage was done. Their followers were shamed and hounded, no longer welcome among their peers. A group of refugees from Lily Dale set out for a place where they could be safe and welcome.

Legend had it, that place was Fox Hollow, a hamlet where misfit paranormals had created a haven for those who didn't belong elsewhere.

Liam pulled himself out of his thoughts and forced himself to pay attention to the road. There were no streetlights out here. Once the sun set, the darkness out here was *really* dark.

Liam knew if he could shift into his fox-self, he'd be able to see just fine. But so far, he hadn't figured out how to drive a car as a fox, and while Dr. Jeffries told him that Fox Hollow was both shifter-aware and shifter-welcoming, Liam didn't want to bet on the tolerance of the county mounties or the state cops.

Just keep driving. Once I'm in Fox Hollow, I'll be safer. Not too much farther now.

Liam had stopped at an ATM for cash and to fill the gas tank before he left Ithaca. He'd loaded up on road food and plenty of coffee so he could drive straight through. That would still get him into Fox Hollow late, but Dr. Jeffries had assured him that no matter what time the call came, he would be over to give Liam the keys and help him get settled.

He passed a sign by the side of the road that read: *Fox Hollow, 10 miles* just when the engine started to rattle and clank. A mile or so later, the noise grew alarmingly worse. Cursing under his breath, Liam pulled off to the side. The state highway didn't have a generous berm, but there hadn't been many cars for the past half hour. He was unlikely to be sideswiped but equally unlikely to have a passer-by offer to help.

Then again, since he hadn't gotten a good look at the Huntsman's face, Liam wouldn't have dared accept help from a random driver.

With a sigh, he grabbed his phone and dug in his wallet for his roadside assistance card, hoping that he wasn't too far from civilization to get a tow that didn't cost a fortune.

"We'll have someone out as quickly as possible," the customer service operator assured him, remaining vexingly light on the details. "Stay where you are, remain in your vehicle to be safe, and we'll send a tow truck."

"Can they tow me to Fox Hollow? That's where I'm headed. I don't know if they have a place that can fix cars."

"You're in luck," she replied. "They do. I'll take care of that for you. Just sit tight."

Liam tapped his thumbs on the steering wheel, feeling twitchy about waiting for a stranger, alone in the dark. While he had heard plenty of people talk about the gorgeous, rugged scenery of the Adirondacks, Liam had apparently skipped over the parts about how dark, empty, and vast the area could seem.

He debated, then discarded, the notion of shifting to his fox to get a sense for his surroundings. He didn't know how quickly the tow truck might arrive, and while the area might tolerate shifters, confronting a hapless driver with a too-knowledgeable fox or a naked man who had just shifted back didn't seem like it was the right way to make new friends.

Showing up naked might make a new friend, but I don't need that kind of trouble on top of everything else. I'm just fine without romantic entanglements for a long, long time. That's what got me into this fuckin' situation in the first place.

Liam didn't dare keep playing music on his phone or from the car radio for fear of draining the batteries. Unfortunately, sitting in the quiet dark just let his thoughts spiral.

How did I not realize what kind of person Kelson was until it was too late? It's not like I was a blushing virgin. I'd had other boyfriends. Been in a few actual relationships. How did Kelson keep me from seeing the real him for so long?

Being cheated on was bad enough. Realizing how much Kelson had lied and manipulated me was worse, but turning me over to a Huntsman to get back at me for confronting him? That's like arranging a hitman. Unforgivable. And if my judgment was bad enough to get me into that mess, how can I ever trust my heart again?

Flashing lights broke Liam out of his gloomy thoughts. The tow truck headed toward him, then did a U-turn and pulled in front of

Liam's car, backing up until it was close enough to hook up the Honda.

The truck driver got out and walked toward Liam, who reluctantly got out of the car. Even though he had called for assistance and it was clear the stranger was a legitimate responder, Liam couldn't help feeling jittery, with his hands sweating, and heart thumping.

Those reactions doubled when he got a good look at the driver.

Oh, just shoot me now. Fuck my life. Why did he have to be so fine?

In the glare of the truck's spotlights, Liam made out all the important details. The man had broad shoulders, strong arms, powerful legs, and a solid chest, standing a good five inches or more over Liam's five-foot-seven frame. Liam had thought he might be saved if the driver was ugly as sin, but he was out of luck. His face was as utterly lickable as the rest of him.

"You called for a tow? Mr. Reynard?"

Liam nodded.

"I'm Russell Lowe—everyone calls me Russ. I own Lowe's Auto Shop in Fox Hollow, and tonight I'm your personal tow truck driver," he said with a broad smile and dimples. The man's sharp cheekbones, full lips, and strong chin were highlighted by dark brown scruff. Liam's gaze traveled upward, surprised at gray hair flecked with brown framing a face that couldn't be older than thirty-five. Green eyes made Liam wonder what kind of shifter Russ might be.

He swallowed hard and might have blushed when he realized Russ seemed to be checking him out too. No matter how attractive his road-side savior might be, Liam'd had enough man trouble to last an eternity, and he sure didn't need more in a new town.

"Yes, I'm Liam Reynard. Just Liam," he said, wishing he could conjure up the natural charm that had always served him well in community theater performances. His fox could be quite dramatic. But now, on the run, scared for his life, and in the dark with a stranger in the middle of nowhere, he couldn't muster his usual flair.

"The engine started making strange noises, and I pulled off. I didn't want to break anything." Liam cringed because he knew next to nothing about cars. *Admitting that takes points off my "man score," doesn't it? Then again, so does being a sports-hating, gay fox shifter twink.*

Well, at thirty, I'd thought my twink days were behind me. But when he compared his own shorter, lithe, dancer build to the solid man-mountain in front of him? *Yeah, twink still fits.*

"I'm glad you stopped the car without waiting for the car to stop you." Russ finally shifted his attention away from Liam and focused on the Civic. "Let's get the tow set up, and then you can ride in the cab with me to Fox Hollow."

He met Liam's gaze, and those green eyes seemed to bore straight through to the fox shifter's soul. "That is where you're going, right?"

Liam's mouth had gone dry. He nodded, cursing himself for reacting to a handsome man like a teenybopper. *Get a grip. I haven't gotten laid in a long time, but it's not like I stopped cleaning the pipes regularly. He is not sex on two legs.*

Russ was *so totally* sex on two legs.

"Yeah. Just moving in. New job. Kinda came up fast." Liam fought the urge to facepalm as his mouth decided to leave without his brain, going from tongue-tied to babbling.

"Well, welcome to Fox Hollow." Russ's smile looked genuine, and he held out his hand for Liam to shake. Liam's scattered wits meant it took a half a second too long to respond.

When he did, as soon as skin met skin, Liam felt a tingle that ran up his arm and straight to his chest. He glanced down, on the odd—and bizarre—chance that Russ had used a prank hand buzzer, but of course there was nothing out of the ordinary.

Nothing except a stunned look on Russ's face that made Liam suspect the stranger had felt the same jolt.

At which point, Liam realized he was still holding Russ's hand.

He released his grip, which had to be the most awkward end to a handshake ever. Liam couldn't remember when he'd made such a fool of himself, at least without alcohol to blame it on.

"It's been a long day," Liam said, and while that didn't begin to cover the truth, it also didn't excuse suddenly losing the ability to function.

Russ smiled, looking a bit perplexed, but still friendly. "I'm sure this isn't how you expected the evening to go. Why don't you get settled in the cab, I'll get the car situated, and we'll head to town. Have you eaten yet?"

The simple concern in Russ's tone and expression threatened to crack Liam's strained-to-the-limit control. He didn't get any vibe that Russ was hitting on him. Hell, for all Liam knew, Russ might be straight, although that handshake made him doubt it. Still, it wasn't good to make assumptions. And what the hell was he doing, even caring whether Russ played for his team when he'd just sworn off ever falling for anyone again?

Liam realized he hadn't answered Russ's question. *I'm an idiot.* "Uh, not really. I got some snacks at the truck stop when I filled the tank, but that was a while ago."

Russ's grin broadened. "I've got you covered. We had a sub sandwich fundraiser at the firehouse today, and there are plenty of leftovers in the fridge at the station. Let's get your car where it needs to go, and then while you fill out paperwork, I'll run over and get you one. Everything else is closed by now," he added apologetically. "Small town and all."

"That would be wonderful. It's kind of you to offer," Liam said, finally finding his wits again.

"Wouldn't be much of a welcome to let you go hungry on your first night in town," Russ replied as he headed to the truck to get the chains. Liam had the distinct feeling Russ would have made the offer to anyone in Liam's situation, which made him think even more highly of the man. Then Russ bent over to secure the car, and Liam got a good look at a jeans-clad perfect ass that fired his imagination.

Let's just hope he doesn't turn around before I can adjust myself, Liam thought, getting a flashback to eighth-grade gym class. He turned away to head for the cab, trying to be discreet as his unruly cock decided to stand at attention.

Thank God for the running board, because Liam didn't want to think about trying to climb into the cab without it. The truck was just like Russ—solid, big, and powerful. The strong arms Liam glimpsed were going to feature in his spank bank at some point, even if Liam had sworn off the real thing.

Alone in the cab, Liam picked up Russ's scent, a combination of aftershave, leather, motor oil, and something earthy that was definitely shifter. *Wolf?* Liam wondered. That would fit with the powerful body and the take-charge attitude. *Might be a gray wolf—explains the hair. Do wolves have green eyes?* He sighed in exasperation in his sudden desire to Google and find out.

Chill. It doesn't matter. He's a wolf; I'm a fox. Not exactly natural enemies, but not automatically compatible, either. And who cares about compatibility. I am not getting involved again. Not gonna get my heart broken. Fuck, I'm running from a guy who wants to kill me because my ex ratted me out. Do I look like I need more man trouble?

He watched Russ in the rearview mirror, pleased that he treated the old Civic carefully, despite the fact that it was not valuable. To Liam, the car was precious, since it was essential transportation and he was going to be short on cash for a while. That care spoke well of Russ, and Liam sighed. *Figures I find a good one when it's too late.*

Russ climbed into the cab, cheeks red from the brisk night air. The puffy down vest made his chest seem even broader while revealing very nice arms clad in a Henley beneath a flannel shirt. "You doing okay?" Russ waited for an answer instead of barreling on, which just made him even more attractive.

Liam nodded. "Yeah, thank you. I didn't expect help to get here so soon."

Russ grinned. "You're only a few miles out of town, and I happened to be on emergency shift tonight." He pulled out onto the dark highway, and Liam tried hard not to stare.

"So you said something about starting a new job? You wouldn't happen to be our new librarian, would you?" Russ asked.

Liam looked up, alarmed that a stranger knew so much about him. "How did you know?"

His companion chuckled. "Small town. You'll get used to it. There aren't a whole lot of jobs that bring people to Fox Hollow. Some open up now and again at the Institute, but they're looking for...special skills."

That made sense. Liam knew he couldn't keep on expecting the worst from everyone, but since someone had tried to kill him tonight, he thought he had cause to be a little freaked out.

"A former professor of mine is on faculty with Fox Institute," Liam replied. "Which is how I heard about the library position. Dr. Jeffries."

"No shit? You know Rich Jeffries? He's a good guy." Russ glanced over to Liam. "So…are you a spook like him?"

Liam chuckled. "A psychic? No. I just took a lot of folklore classes from him when he taught at Ithaca. Turns out he understood what he was teaching on a much deeper level."

The Spiritualists that fled Lily Dale founded the Fox Institute—named for the unfortunate Fox Sisters—as a place to educate, research parapsychological phenomena, and gather like-minded seekers.

"You went to Ithaca? Good school. That's pretty countryside down in the Finger Lakes area."

"Yeah, it is," Liam agreed. "I liked it there." He couldn't keep the wistfulness out of his voice. The day had started to catch up to him. Liam hoped Russ didn't ask why he left.

"So…how do you know Dr. Jeffries?" Liam asked since they had time to kill.

"Rich is the Institute liaison for community events, like the arts festival and the Fall Fling—or the firehouse fundraiser. Probably how he knew about the library opening."

"You're a firefighter?" Liam raised an eyebrow.

"Yeah. Small town, remember?" Russ replied with a smirk. "Fox Hollow has a lot more going on than you might think for a town its size, but none of that happens by accident. Our folks step up to the plate, and that means we all wear at least three or four hats."

"So you own the auto body shop, and you run the tow service, and you fight fires?" Liam was used to academics shouldering multiple roles, but he didn't think the same was true outside of a campus environment. *Damn. Every time he opens his mouth, he's more impressive.*

Russ chuckled and blushed adorably.

No. Not "adorably." Just kinda cute. Must. Not. Notice.

"Like I said, small town. Fox Hollow is a very special place. I hope you'll like it."

"I hope so too," Liam replied, wishing with all his heart for it to be true.

"So, you're getting in late, and it's still before the tourist season starts. Do you have a place to stay lined up?"

Liam nodded. "Dr. Jeffries said he'd taken care of it. I'm supposed to call him when I get there, no matter what time it is."

Russ nodded. "Good. I'll get your car tucked away, get you fed, and then we'll give Rich a call."

Liam perked up when they came to a sign welcoming them to Fox Hollow. He saw a restaurant and an ice cream shop, then what looked like a general store, and more buildings he'd need to get a better look at in daylight. His research had shown him the tourist brochure highlights, but the real thing looked even better. Liam found that despite how exhausted he was, exploring tomorrow sounded like fun.

"Here we are," Russ said, pulling the tow truck into a car care station that took up a whole corner on the main street. Liam saw a gas station, repair bays, and a neat cinderblock building offering tires, wipers, and other auto essentials.

"Stay put," Russ told him as he went to open one of the bay doors. "It's a lot warmer in here than out there."

Liam felt the day catching up to him. The warm cab felt safe and comfortable, and he hated the thought of leaving. Russ had managed to make him not feel like the new kid in town, but as soon as he stepped outside, reality would crowd back in.

Russ backed the truck up, and then went around to ease the Civic into one of the bays. He shut the big door and brought the truck to the front of the shop, where he parked and then jumped out to open up the front door.

"C'mon inside. I'll let you start filling out the paperwork and go get you that sandwich."

Liam knew he probably should protest, but he was tired, hungry, alone in a strange place, and just a few hours ago, someone had tried to kill him. As the shock wore off and the reality of his situation sank in, Liam felt his stomach flip and his hands shake.

Russ ushered him into his office, which looked as tidy and straightforward as the man. "Have a seat," he offered, indicating a plastic chair. Russ gathered several forms and handed them to Liam along with a pen and a clipboard.

"Allergies?"

"What?" Liam asked, confused at the non-sequitur.

"For the sandwich. Anything you don't eat?"

Again, Russ's casual thoughtfulness touched Liam, even though he knew he needed to harden his heart. "I'm pretty easy," he replied, then wanted to facepalm. *Oh God, did I say that out loud?*

"I mean…I'm not allergic, and I'm not picky," he covered. "Sorry… it's been a very long day." *That was the understatement of the year.*

Russ didn't comment on the obvious double meaning, although that totally-not-adorable blush indicated that he'd noticed. *He noticed, and he's not being weird about it. Does that mean he's gay or bi? Or just extraordinarily secure?*

"I'll be right back," Russ promised. "I'll lock the door—although crime in Fox Hollow is pretty much non-existent. We watch out for each other here."

Liam busied himself filling out the paperwork, and stopped when he realized he didn't know his new address. After everything, it just suddenly seemed like too much. He covered his face with both hands, panting, trying not to have a full meltdown.

"Don't scare the nice wolf shifter," he muttered to himself. "Hold it together. Just a little longer."

Liam drew a few long, shuddering breaths and got himself back under control. He managed to fill out everything except his address, and it occurred to him that Russ had a good chance of knowing it. Small town, and all that.

He hoped he didn't look twitchy when Russ returned. His fox could be dramatic, but now it was the wily side that sustained him, the cunning for which foxes were famous. Head, not heart needed to rule —at least until he was in private.

He heard the door open, and Russ entered in a rush of cold air. "Miss me?" he joked.

Liam covered an instant of panic with a fake smile. *Actually, I did.* "I was immersed in these riveting forms," he deadpanned.

Russ put a can of Coke, a small bag of chips, and a wrapped sub sandwich on the desk. "All yours. It's a club sandwich—local favorite. Nothing fancy, but lots of good stuff. Our bestseller."

Liam handed off the clipboard and pulled his chair up to the desk, surprised how hungry he was now that food was in front of him. He feared that he might be too nervous to eat, but apparently he'd reached the point where self-preservation took over. He would have sworn it was the best he'd ever tasted. "This is awesome. What do I owe you?"

Russ shook his head. "Like I said—it was a leftover. Welcome to Fox Hollow."

"Thank you."

Russ moved around the office, and it seemed to Liam that the other man was killing time, transferring his paperwork to the next-day queue, tidying his desk—anything to give Liam time to eat without feeling rushed. The no-nonsense kindness threatened to undo Liam, and he had to look away before he lost it.

"Do you want to call Rich now?" Russ asked when Liam gathered up his trash and sank it in the wastebasket next to the desk. It took Liam a moment to realize Russ meant Dr. Jeffries.

Liam checked his phone. Nearly midnight, but not too terrible. "Yes. I have his number."

"Give him a call. I think I know where he's going to put you, and I'll walk you over."

"You know where I'm going to live?" *Which is weird, since I don't.* Liam had thought it was a possibility, but having his guess confirmed felt a little...odd.

"Sure. There's a bungalow behind the library that was the original library long ago. Walter Tollson—the previous librarian—lived there until he passed away last winter. Rich'll have the key."

Liam called Jeffries, and the brief call confirmed Russ's guess. He promised to meet him at the bungalow.

Russ grinned. "Come on—it isn't far."

Liam grabbed his laptop bag and duffel out of his car then followed Russ. He reluctantly left the warmth of the office and flinched as a cold wind knifed through his too-thin jacket.

"You do have a heavier coat, I hope."

Liam nodded. "Yeah—in my bag. Boots and hat and everything."

"Good. Because winter isn't quite over yet, and it'll be back before you know it."

Liam followed him across the street and behind the brick two-story building with the *Library* sign in front. A walkway led to a courtyard in the back and a small bungalow in the Arts and Crafts style. All that mattered to Liam right now was that he had a place to spend the night.

He'd sort everything out tomorrow.

"Liam. I'm so glad you made it here safely."

Liam turned at the familiar voice. Dr. Richard Jeffries strode up the walk, nearly unrecognizable in his coat and scarf. "Dr. Jeffries. Sorry to bother you so late."

"Pfft. No bother. I told you to call, and I meant it. I'm beyond happy to have you here with us." The older man glanced from Liam to Russ. "Did you have car trouble?" The worry in his eyes told Liam his friend might have had a premonition about Liam being in danger.

"His car gave out on him about ten miles from town," Russ said, slapping Jeffries on the shoulder in greeting with a gloved hand. "I towed him in, got him fed, and now he's all yours."

"Thank you," Liam spoke up, surprised at how much he hated to see Russ go. "For everything."

"Sure," Russ replied, with a twinkle in those green eyes. "Welcome to the neighborhood." He waved then headed back the way they came, and Liam realized too late he was watching the other man walk away.

"Russ is a great guy," Dr. Jeffries said. "Sorry that you had trouble, but you were in good hands."

Liam tried hard not to think about Russ's hands or all the other delicious parts of his body. "He saved my bacon. I would have had a cold night in the car."

Dr. Jeffries moved past him and unlocked the door, then went to turn on lights. "I came over earlier and got the furnace turned on so it would be warm in here. Double checked that the pipes hadn't frozen. Left you some doughnuts for breakfast and a can of freshly-ground java for the coffee maker. Made the bed up with clean sheets too. There are some travel-size toiletries courtesy of the last hotel I stayed in. We left Walter's furniture because we didn't know what might be needed. You can make your own decisions on that later."

It was all suddenly too much. Liam sank down on the couch, barely holding it together. The emotional whiplash between Kelson's betrayal, the Huntsman's intent to kill him, and now the unexpected kindness of both Russ and Dr. Jeffries was too much.

"Liam, is everything okay?"

Tomorrow, Liam owed his mentor the truth—at least about the Huntsman. He owed Jeffries that much, in case Liam accidentally brought danger to the town that offered him sanctuary. But not tonight. Liam refused to break down because he was afraid that if he did, he might not be able to pull himself back together.

"Yeah. Just not my best day," he managed. "Thank you. This is all so much more than I could have hoped for, and...I'm a little over-whelmed."

Dr. Jeffries didn't push, but from his expression, Liam figured the man could tell there was more he hadn't said. *Hello? He's psychic.*

"Get some sleep," Jeffries said in a kind tone. "How about if I come by at ten and show you around the library, then give you the town tour?"

Liam nodded, swallowing hard. "I'd like that. Sounds great."

"I'll let myself out and lock the door behind me. The key is on the kitchen table. Good night, Liam. See you in the morning."

Liam heard the door close. A few minutes later, he walked out to double-check the lock and put the key in his wallet since he'd left his keyring with the Civic.

He found the bedroom, said another silent "thank you" to Jeffries for the bedding and toiletries, then stripped out of his clothes, slid beneath the blankets, and tried to ignore the fact that he was sleeping in a strange house, in a new town, in a borrowed bed. This morning, he'd been in his own cozy apartment, in a place he knew and loved, with a job and friends and a plan for his future.

And now, his world had turned inside-out. It was all too much, and Liam refused to feel ashamed as he cried himself to sleep.

2

RUSS

"You're here early, for a Saturday. I can't remember the last time I saw you here at eight."

Russ snorted. "Unlike my sleepyhead baby brother." He slid out from under Liam's Civic, flat on his back on a garage creeper. He looked up at a face that nearly mirrored his own, except for darker hair and fewer eye crinkles. Drew Lowe was Russ's pain-in-the-ass sibling, best friend, partner in hijinks, and co-owner of Lowe's Automotive Care.

He was also the only member of his birth pack who stuck with Russ when his parents threw him out for being gay.

"Where'd you get the beater?" Drew nodded toward the old Honda.

Russ had already bristled defensively before he caught himself. *Wait, what? Why am I ready to fight over an insult to Liam's car?* "Our new librarian had car trouble last night on his way into town. I towed him and promised we'd get it fixed."

"You sure it's worth it?" Drew asked skeptically.

Once again, Russ fought down an uncharacteristic surge of protectiveness over the car, which was just downright weird. "It's not a bad little car, and these things last forever. Looks like he's done a lot to take care of it. Fortunately, he didn't try to keep going when it acted up. The damage isn't too bad."

He shimmied under the car again, and pushed any questions about his odd reactions out of his thoughts to focus on the job at hand.

"So...new librarian."

"Yep."

"Younger than Walter?"

Russ chuckled. "Oh, yeah."

"Wait...is he cute?"

"Drew—"

"That's an objective question."

"It totally isn't."

"Guess I'll have to go check him out for myself. This town could use some fresh meat."

Russ was out from under the car and had a grease-stained fist clenching his brother's T-shirt before his brain registered what was going on. "Don't talk about him like that."

Drew looked at Russ like he'd lost his marbles and raised both hands in appeasement. Belatedly, Russ realized he was still holding Drew's shirt, which now had black, finger-shaped streaks. He let go and took a step back. "Sorry."

"Shit. He's your mate!" Drew exclaimed, wide-eyed with amazement.

Russ met Drew's gaze and felt panic thrum through him. "No. No way."

"Dude, the last time you almost took a swing at me was in fifth grade when I broke your game controller. You just defended his *car*. I made a pervy comment, and your wolf almost went for my throat. Oh, my God."

Russ stumbled more than walked to a plastic chair inside his office, and dropped heavily into it. Fortunately, it was still early, so they didn't have any witnesses to their little spat. Drew tossed him a shop rag to wipe off his hands, and Russ cleaned up distractedly, then folded the cloth. He wanted to argue, but the truth of Drew's observation stirred his wolf, who just seemed smug.

"No. It can't be!"

Drew crossed his arms and smirked. "Go ahead. I want to see you argue yourself out of this."

Russ shook his head. "Fated mates aren't real."

"They aren't common. But you know the story about Grandma and Grandpa Lowe."

Russ closed his eyes in denial. Of course he knew the story. How many times had they heard it? She'd been a waitress at a diner. He'd been a mechanic, just passing through town. When their fingers brushed as she passed him a plate of cherry pie, they had both known they were fated mates. They ran off to Vegas that night and had their first pups not long after and were still going strong half a century later.

He clenched his fists, still fighting against Drew's observation. *I said I wasn't going to let myself in for heartbreak again. Not after how much it hurt to lose Anthony.*

"Russ, it's been two years. Don't you think Anthony would want you to be happy?"

This time, Drew stayed out of reach, backing up another step at Russ's low growl. "You're out of line."

"Am I?" Drew shot back. "I know you were happy with Anthony. But he's gone. You haven't been yourself since then."

"Because I buried my husband!"

Drew's expression and tone were comforting, but his body language told Russ his brother wasn't going to back down. "You didn't have to bury yourself with him."

Russ surged to his feet, but Drew's cocked eyebrow stopped him in his place. Drew usually let Russ take the lead, but he could be stubborn as all hell when the fight was worth it, and it looked like Drew had decided to stand his ground.

Russ took a couple of deep breaths. Even now, just thinking about that night put a lump in his throat and brought tears to his eyes. He'd been on emergency duty with the fire department when a car wrapped around a tree after it hit black ice. Dispatch hadn't realized who the victim was when they put out the call for an assist.

Some of the details of that awful night were still spotty. But not the shock and horror of recognizing the car, crowding forward as Anthony's body was eased out of the driver's seat, and the pity in the EMTs' eyes as the severity of the injuries became apparent.

Russ remembered the random thought that had gone through his mind when the doctor called time of death. *If we had been fated mates, I don't think I would have survived.*

"I can't," he said, hating how broken his voice sounded. Dammit—it had taken two years to start functioning again, to feel present in the moment instead of like he was drifting through a never-ending fog. To not feel guilty about laughing or enjoying a sunny day, or feeling horny—even though he met that need by himself. To not feel guilty for being *alive.*

"Can we not try to solve this right now?" Russ managed, as he shut the office door and sat back down. "Liam just moved here last night. And...even though he didn't say so, I have a feeling that he's worried about something."

Drew leaned against the wall, frowning as if he were parsing out what Russ really meant. Russ knew that Drew had a lifetime of experience watching his big brother and learning his tells. They'd always been close, and that translated into a sense of each other that bordered on telepathy.

"You think he's in trouble?"

Russ paused, but his wolf surged forward. "Yes. I don't know why or how, but my wolf is sure of it."

Drew shrugged. "Wolves are all about non-verbal language. You probably picked up on Liam's scent. Is Liam a shifter?"

Russ just stared at him. "I'm not sure. He said he came here because Rich Jeffries told him about the job—turns out Jeffries was his professor in college."

"Interesting," Drew mused. He walked over to pour himself a cup of coffee and held out a cup to Russ, who nodded, accepting it like a peace offering.

Russ ran back over the events of the previous night, sifting his wolf instincts through his human mind. "Okay—I'd guess Liam is about thirty. But all he had in his car was a duffel and his computer bag. He's moving here—permanently—with less stuff than most people take on vacation. But I didn't get the impression he was poor—not if he went to Ithaca. And if he got hired to run the library, then he's got to have a master's degree, right? But everything he owns fits in two bags?"

"Maybe there's more in the trunk."

Russ's gaze flitted to the side, avoiding Drew.

"Seriously? You broke into his trunk?"

"I had the key."

"Russ..."

He huffed and then rolled his eyes. "Fine. Yes, I did. And no, it just had the usual junk, but not like you'd pack a car to move."

"Maybe he's got a moving van coming after he gets situated."

Russ shrugged. "Maybe. But he didn't mention it, even at the bungalow."

"Why would he be in trouble? What kind of trouble wouldn't have thrown a red flag on hiring him?" Drew asked.

"Jeffries seemed concerned about him too," Russ said, as he began to see some of the previous night's actions in a new light.

He leaned forward, cradling his cup in his hands. "I'm fucked. I can't get the guy out of my head, Drew," Russ confessed.

"Tell me all about it," Drew said. "Except for the fucking part."

Russ glared at him. "We didn't fuck."

"TMI, bro." Drew perched on the corner of the desk. "If anyone asks why we're in here, we'll call it a management meeting. Kerrie's at the front desk, so we're not keeping any customers waiting. Now, spill."

Russ recounted everything that had happened, from the dispatch call to the ride back to town, including the sandwich incident and walking Liam to his new home.

"You are so screwed," Drew commiserated. "So what you're telling me is that within the first two hours of meeting Liam, you rescued him, comforted him, fed him, and made sure he had safe shelter? Could your wolf howl any louder?"

No, he couldn't, Russ thought sourly. *His wolf hadn't stopped pacing since he'd left Liam at the bungalow, and it had been a battle of wills not to give in and keep watch over him during the night. Only by convincing his wolf that humans might consider such actions as "stalkerish" and thereby scare Liam off for good did he get his wolf to back off.*

Russ realized his hands were shaking. "I'm not ready for this, Drew."

"Your wolf is."

"My wolf thinks you can deal with problems by biting them or peeing on them."

"You mean you can't?" Drew's shit-eating grin was oddly reassuring, an unspoken affirmation that everything would be okay.

"I don't even know if he's a shifter. He said he wasn't a psychic—he just knew Jeffries from the folklore classes Rich used to teach."

"Hmm. That doesn't keep *Rich* from knowing whether Liam is a shifter. And didn't this whole thing happen awfully fast?" Drew asked. "I thought Rich was complaining at poker night last week that one of his Institute colleagues was trying to push his favored candidate for the job, even without the right credentials. And now Liam's not just hired—but he's here, moved in, and ready to start?"

Russ met his gaze. "You think maybe Rich picked up on whatever trouble Liam might have had and offered him a lifeline?"

"Sure seems likely."

Not like I can ask, or that Rich would tell me. But I hope that if Liam does have trouble brewing, Rich was able to lend a hand.

"This guy also has you being more Libra than usual," Drew pointed out. With all the psychics in town, even the shifters took things like astrological signs and tarot readings seriously. "Romantic, loyal, protective—and always overthinking things."

Russ just growled, because Drew was right and he knew it.

"When's Liam's birthday? What's his sign?"

"How would I know?" Russ grumbled.

"You looked at his license to do the repairs, didn't you?" Drew grabbed the paperwork off Russ's desk and glanced at the photocopy of Liam's license. "Oh-ho! Looky here! He's a Leo…your perfect zodiac match. Wow, there's a surprise."

Russ snatched the papers back and opened his mouth to argue when the intercom on his desk buzzed. "There's a Liam Reynard here to see you."

"Thanks. I'll be right there," Russ replied.

"Ohh…do I get to see him too?" His brother asked, managing to channel what Russ considered Drews's pesky ten-year-old self.

"Behave."

"Russ and Liam sitting in a tree—"

Russ snapped the hand towel at Drew, who dodged out of the way. "Seriously, Drew—"

Drew clapped him on the shoulder. "I will be the soul of discretion."

The door opened, and Liam stepped inside.

"Wow—you must be the guy Russ was just telling me about," Drew said with a big grin. He thrust out a hand to shake Liam's. "I'm Drew, his younger and better-looking brother."

The next time he shifts I'm going to make sure he tangles with a skunk. Russ took a deep breath and tried not to look mortified. Liam smiled, then frowned, as if trying to figure out what was going on.

"Liam. Don't mind Drew—he was just leaving," Russ added emphasis on the last word. He could hear Drew laughing all the way down the hall. "Siblings," he muttered, then turned his attention back to Liam, hoping he could reclaim any semblance of cool.

"So...sleep well?" Russ asked the first thing that came to mind and groaned inwardly at what came out of his mouth.

"Yeah, I did. For once," Liam replied. "Didn't expect to—new place and all—but I guess I was pretty tired after everything that happened."

Liam didn't look like a man who had slept soundly. Likely, if whatever was bothering Liam was more than a passing inconvenience. His eyes were shadowed, he held himself like he might need to run at any moment, and in Russ's imagination, he could almost see a tail swishing impatiently.

Fox shifter, his wolf supplied. *Can't you tell by his scent?*

The scent that Russ picked up was burnt orange and cloves, with an earthy, musky undertone that went straight to Russ's cock. Now that he looked at Liam, he could see the fox in the other man's graceful movements, lithe build, and the slightly tilted, amber eyes that would look amazing outlined with a smidge of kohl. Russ had never been big on guyliner, but on Liam, it would be sexy as fuck.

Russ cleared his throat, realizing they were both staring at each other. *Awkward.*

"Um, I don't have your car ready yet. Sorry. I came in early to start on it, but I'm waiting on parts, and then my brother showed up—"

"That's okay. I don't think I'm going to need it for a while," Liam assured him, looking as unnerved as Russ felt.

Does he sense that we're mates too? Will he want me? Or will he be upset I'm not a fox? Holy fuck—why am I even worrying about this?

But Russ knew why. His wolf wasn't going to let this go, not if there was any chance of making Liam his. As much as Russ had loved Anthony—and he had, with all his heart—he'd always wondered how it might be different with a true fated mate. If the overwhelming strength of this initial stage was anything to go by, Russ couldn't imagine the intensity of being even more closely connected.

"Just checking in?" Russ asked with a smile.

"I wanted to thank you again, and make sure you didn't need anything else from me. I was kinda jumbled last night."

"I've got everything I need to handle the repair. You left me the insurance card. I think we're set." Russ looked in the box for Liam's car keys and didn't see them. "I should have your keys right here."

Liam pulled out his phone, tapped the screen, and something chirped from Russ's inbox.

"Did you do that?" Russ asked.

Liam gave a sheepish smile. "Yeah. I'm always forgetting where I left my phone or my keys, so I got those GPS Tiles to help me find them. Comes in handy."

Russ pulled the keys from under a piece of paper and saw the small, slim square dangling from the keyring. "Is that what made the noise?"

"Yep. And if I have my keys and lose my phone, it works in reverse too. I put one on all my keys. Saves time, aggravation, and my blood pressure."

"Huh. I guess I learn something new every day," Russ replied. "I'm glad you stopped by."

Liam nodded, looking charmingly flustered. "Good. Well, you have my number. Dr. Jeffries is going to take me through the library and show me around town. I need to get back to the house. I just…wanted to stop in."

"Thanks. I'll call soon."

He feels it! Russ's wolf celebrated, doing a little victory strut in his mind.

We don't know that for sure. Russ pointed out as he waved goodbye and watched Liam walk out. Russ would have to be comatose to not sense the chemistry between them or the sheer sexual attraction that had his cock hard from a whiff of Liam's scent.

But they were people, not animals, and that meant that even for fated mates, both parties had to agree. More importantly, they had to want the pairing. Just because Russ's wolf thought Liam was signed-sealed-and-delivered didn't mean squat in the real world.

The rest of the day passed in a blur. The parts would have taken a week by mail—the downside to being in a little town in the middle of nowhere—but Russ got his pilot friend, Justin, to bring the order back from another run up to Saranac Lake. He felt inordinately pleased to be able to finish the car repairs sooner than expected, and Russ knew his wolf preened at what it considered to be a mating gift.

It's not a gift. He's paying for the repairs.

You could make it a gift.

He wouldn't accept. Humans do things differently.

I'm aware. A freshly-killed rabbit is a much better gift than a stinky car.

That would get me arrested, not laid.

We would make sure it was a real rabbit, not one of the neighbors.

Thank you so much. Not helping.

Russ's wolf padded off to sulk, and Russ welcomed the silence as he finished a couple of tune-ups, custom-ordered a set of tires for a client, and sent in the paperwork for new snow equipment. The spring snow had barely melted, but it would be fall again in the blink of an eye, and early orders were more likely to get filled before demand made essentials scarce.

He managed to push Liam out of his thoughts for a couple of hours, at least until the man himself came walking in after Kerrie called to tell him his car was ready.

"How did you get it finished so fast?" Liam asked, then looked at Russ like he was some kind of hero.

Russ shrugged. "A buddy of mine had to fly up to Saranac for business, and he brought the parts back with him, so we didn't have to wait on snail mail."

"Wow. Thank you. I appreciate you calling in a favor for me."

Russ snorted. "Since Justin's one of my poker buddies, it's more like I'll be doing him a favor in return by not whupping his ass at cards...at least, on the first hand," he added with a grin.

Liam looked both interested and hesitant. Russ felt more sure than ever that something—or someone—had scared Liam badly. He didn't think either of them were up for anything more than being friends right now. *But when you're the new guy in town, and you don't know anyone, it's good to have a friend, right?*

"Well, thank you for everything," Liam said, meeting Russ's gaze with those fascinating, amber eyes. Russ had sworn he was going to keep his distance, but Liam's eyes could make a man forget those kinds of promises.

"You're very welcome. And I, er, threw in a tune-up—on the house —to make sure everything keeps working right," Russ said.

Liam seemed to relax, just a bit. "Thank you, again."

"Would you like to get coffee sometime?" Russ blurted. His wolf gave a smug chuff, managing to get words out of Russ's mouth before his human brain caught up.

Liam looked uncertain, then managed a hesitant but real smile. "Sure. Dr. Jeffries told me a lot about Fox Hollow on our walk, but I've still got lots of questions."

"Drew and I aren't natives, but we've been here for more than ten years, so I think I can come up with some of those answers, and if I can't, Sherrie and Nelson who own Bear Necessity Coffee can fill you in," Russ replied, aware that he was smiling broadly and probably looked like a maniac. He hadn't smiled like that since... He fought not to let the light go out at the thought of Anthony's death.

I don't want to explain Anthony's death, not right off the bat. And I don't want Liam to think anything he did caused my mood change. Hell, it's just coffee.

He is our mate. Make it more than coffee. I will get a rabbit if I need to, his wolf offered.

Russ chose to ignore his wolf for the moment. "Tomorrow's

Sunday. The library is usually closed. Do you want to meet up in the morning?"

Liam nodded. "That would be great. And I'd like to hear your impressions of the library and the community programs and the festivals. Dr. Jeffries told me a lot, and I've read the websites, but I need to know the lay of the land, so to speak, before I wade into planning for the summer."

"I can fill you in." Russ's smile brightened naturally. The community programs put on by the library and the Institute were some of the things he and Drew enjoyed the most about Fox Hollow.

"Okay then," Liam said, with a shy smile that made Russ swallow hard. "I'll see you tomorrow. Say, nine?"

"Nine's good."

Since Kerrie had already handled check-out, Russ opened the bay door and walked Liam to his car, parked just outside, then waved as he drove away. Russ glanced around, but neither Jimmy nor Steve, his other mechanics, seemed to be paying any attention. That helped, since Drew—and probably Kerrie—were going to be paying a lot more attention than Russ wanted. They had both made some subtle and not-so-subtle comments about learning to enjoy life again after loss.

That sort of thing always seemed like good advice—until someone aimed it at him.

Since it was Saturday, they closed the shop early. They weren't open on Sundays even during tourist season unless there was an emergency, which could happen since Fox Hollow was a helluva long way from the next nearest auto center. Russ was glad to have the time off, not just to have coffee with Liam, but also to sort out his jumbled thoughts.

He cleaned up his bay as Jimmy and Steve finished straightening their area and wished them both a good rest of the weekend. Then he changed out of his coveralls and folded them up to take with him and wash. Drew had already headed out to the cabin they shared to get ready for poker night, which generally involved beer, burgers, and snacks.

Tonight, Russ felt a restlessness that for once didn't have anything to do with his wolf. His thoughts were in turmoil, and his heart felt pulled in too many directions. He saw Kerrie off and locked up the shop, then got in his Grand Cherokee and drove away.

Russ parked at the far edge of the lot behind the grocery store and paused to look over the old cemetery that ran behind the Unitarian church. He could easily have walked since the auto shop was across the street, but he wasn't sure what shape he'd be in when he did what he needed to do and didn't want to run into anyone.

Russ caught himself stalling and sighed, then forced himself to open the car door. The late afternoon wind had a chill to it as the sun sank on the horizon, still leaving plenty of light to navigate the old graveyard. He wasn't worried about ghosts. Russ didn't doubt that ghosts were real—his wolf easily sensed spirits when any were around. But with an institute full of psychics and mediums just a few blocks away, Fox Hollow's ghosts were probably the best tended anywhere except Lily Dale, and any spirits that caused trouble were promptly handled.

The old part of the graveyard was behind the church, while the newer burials were in the "overflow" section as Russ had always thought of it. He'd chosen a lot here for Anthony because it was closer than the modern memorial garden outside town, and Russ had always preferred headstones to the "mow over" flat plaques.

In all the time Anthony and I were together, we never discussed funerals or burial wishes. We thought we had all the time in the world.

Russ had never expected to be widowed at thirty-three.

His feet knew the way without him needing to think about the path. That first year, he had come at least once a week, sometimes more often. It made him feel a little less lonely, even though he hoped Anthony's spirit had moved on to somewhere peaceful and happy.

He'd thought about asking a medium to see if he could say goodbye but chickened out every time. The spiritualists with the Fox Institute were the real deal; Russ didn't doubt that. But part of him would rather take comfort from the times he thought he sensed Anthony's spirit than know for sure. From the reaction his wolf had at those times when Russ suspected an otherworldly presence, he felt pretty sure Anthony still kept an eye on him. Which was another reason he needed to have this conversation.

Seeing the granite headstone made Russ tear up every time. He'd wanted to make it a double monument, with room for his information when the time came. Drew had argued loudly against that, partly because Russ was so young, and partly, Russ suspected, out of superstitious fear that it might hurry his passing. Russ had relented, figuring that Anthony was past caring, but Drew cared passionately, and so he erred on the side of comforting the living. Still, he'd bought the plot beside Anthony's, something he hadn't mentioned to his brother.

The black granite stone made the chiseled inscription stand out clearly. *Anthony Moretti* at the top, then two intertwined hearts and his birth and death dates. Beneath that, *Beloved husband, gone too soon. Always remembered.*

Russ didn't try to hide the tears as he reached in his pocket and withdrew a small stone he'd picked up to lay on the top of the headstone, an old custom. Then he sank to his haunches as if that put him on eye-level somehow.

"Tony, I don't know what to do," Russ confided. "I miss you something fierce. I always figured we'd get old and bald together, move to Florida, and yell at the kids to get off our lawn. Never this." His voice caught, and he dragged his arm across his eyes.

"I swore I wasn't going to look for anyone else after I lost you. How could anyone compare? You were it for me. And I didn't look, I swear. But my wolf thinks we've met our fated mate. You know I never believed in that. You brought it up once, and I shut you down because I thought it was just a legend. I thought we were pretty perfect together, all on our own."

He sniffed back tears. "But now, I don't know what to think. It's all new, but it's very real and a little overwhelming. Maybe it won't work out...but my wolf isn't going to give it up. So...I need to ask your blessing," Russ went on. "I was always faithful to you. And I haven't even given anyone a second glance. But this time...I'm attracted. Strongly."

He felt his cheeks heat as if he were confessing infidelity. "It's more than that. There's a connection that is so deep it feels hard-wired. I think he feels it too. And I just wanted to talk it over with you, so you knew I hadn't forgotten you. I'm never going to be 'over' you. But I'm lonely and Drew, and my wolf won't shut up until I give this a try. Can you forgive me? And give me a sign if you're still here?"

Russ waited, listening in the silent cemetery. The breeze kicked up, rustling his hair, and carried on it a hint of leather and bay rum, both scents he associated with Anthony.

"Thank you," he murmured brokenly. "You know I'll always love you." He pressed his fingers to his lips, then to the cold granite.

Russ stood, murmuring goodbye, and taking a ragged breath to collect himself. Movement at the tree line behind the cemetery caught his eye, and he saw a flash of red.

Was that a fox? Could it have been Liam?

Foxes were as common up here as bear, bobcats, and "regular" wolves. Most of the animals in the forest weren't shifters, although the longer someone lived in Fox Hollow, the harder it became to remember that. Then again, if the bond that seemed to be forming between him and Liam was truly as strong as he suspected, it might not be odd at all for Liam to be drawn to a place where Russ was experiencing strong emotions. There was no good way to ask, but Russ promised himself he'd be alert for opportunities to confirm his hunch.

By the time he got to the cabin, Russ felt like he'd gotten his emotions under control. He parked and took a couple of deep breaths before he got the case of beer out of the back. The cabin had belonged to a friend of their grandfather's, his "quiet place" to go fishing. Sometimes their grandfather would bring them with him when he and his buddy came up for the weekend.

Then Russ grew up and came out, and his family fractured. Drew sided with him; the rest of the pack didn't. His grandfather's friend must have disagreed because he found Russ and offered him a good deal on the cabin, which he wasn't using anymore. Russ and Drew needed a place to live, and that just sealed the decision to move to Fox Hollow.

They built onto the cabin, expanding it and modernizing, to make it a year-round home instead of a vacation place, and adding enough elbow room that they weren't tripping over each other.

When Russ and Anthony married, Russ moved into Anthony's house, a tidy little two-story closer to town. Then the wreck happened only three years later. Anthony had left the house to Russ, but he couldn't bear to live there alone.

Drew invited him back to the cabin, Russ sold the house, and here they were—two bachelor brothers. Maybe it was the need to keep pack close, or just wanting his family, but Russ had found the same safe space in the cabin to heal after Anthony's death that he and Drew had both found when they'd left home.

Time to stop thinking, play a little poker, and chill out, he thought, hefting the case of beer as he juggled his keys. Drew saw him coming and opened the door.

"Took you long enough. I thought you had already bought the beer?" Drew groused as Russ set his burden down on the floor and took off his coat and shoes in the entranceway. Then he carried the beer to the kitchen and moved bottles into the cooler of ice Drew had ready.

"Took a while to lock up," Russ replied, not looking away from his task.

"You went to see Anthony." Drew's quiet voice stopped Russ mid-motion.

Russ closed his eyes and swallowed, then nodded. "Yeah. You know me pretty well."

"Did it help?" Drew understood. He sounded concerned.

"I think so. But, there's nothing to tell yet about Liam and me. I'm probably jumping to all kinds of conclusions," Russ replied, and his wolf growled, quick to contradict him.

"I don't think so. Neither do you."

"Unfortunately, we have absolutely no idea what Liam thinks." Russ sensed mutual attraction, but that didn't mean Liam would be open to exploring more than friendship.

"So...find out."

"We're having coffee together tomorrow morning."

Drew slapped him on the shoulder as Russ finished with the cooler and stood up. "Good for you!"

Russ rolled his eyes. "Thanks for your support." He looked around the kitchen at the bowls of chips and containers of dips, then inhaled the smell of pizza baking. "And thanks for getting things set up for tonight."

"No problem. I even got the table ready. The guys should be here soon. Go take a shower. You stink."

Russ headed for the bathroom, stripped off his shirt, then tossed it and his coveralls into the laundry basket. Upgrading the cabin's appliances and bathroom had been the priorities when he and Drew had first moved in, projects they had taken on just as soon as they could afford them. Russ fully believed that a hot shower with good water pressure could make up for a lot of shitty things that happened during an average day.

He stood under the water, letting it sluice away grease, sweat, and tears, then lathered up. The eucalyptus-mint soap was an indulgence, purchased from a local maker, but it was a luxury worth the splurge. He scrubbed his hands, knowing that traces of grease always lingered around his nails and in the creases of his knuckles.

Maybe I'm too blue-collar for a guy like Liam. Anthony was a fishing guide. We were on equal footing. I have a degree, not that anyone would guess. And I like to read a lot. Will that count?

His hand fell to his cock, thinking about how good Liam looked when he had dropped by the shop. Red hair, short on the sides, longer on top. Those slightly tilted amber eyes, imagined with a bit of kohl to set them off. Liam's slender build would feel perfect in his arms, lean and strong, graceful like a dancer. He was a nice height to tuck under Russ's chin. Just the right size to lift into his arms and fuck against the wall, with his ankles locked behind Russ's back.

His hand moved quickly, stroking his hard cock. He imagined having Liam in the shower with him, pictured dropping to his knees and nuzzling the ginger thatch around Liam's prick. He imagined it being slender and uncut, just perfect to deep throat. Being enveloped by Liam's scent and the warmth of his groin, tasting his pre-come— just thinking about it had Russ gasping as he spurted over his fist, coming harder than he had in a long time.

He watched his jizz go down the drain as his heart pounded, and he panted for air. *Holy fuck, that was intense—and Liam wasn't even here.*

Russ waited to feel guilty. After Anthony died, it had taken months before Russ even felt the urge to jack off. Thinking about Anthony hurt too much and picturing any handsome stranger from real life felt like cheating, so he'd fantasized about the actors from their favorite porn, something they'd enjoyed watching together. He'd kept to that even after his body woke up again, having zero interest in looking for a hook-up or a date. Once in a great while, Anthony would show up in a sex dream. Russ would wake with sticky boxer-briefs and tears still wet on his face. That hadn't happened in months.

But for once, he didn't feel guilty. Instead, Russ felt relaxed, sated—the way sex was supposed to feel. Not even embarrassed about rubbing one out as he thought about a man he'd just met. Being intimate with Liam felt right, inevitable.

I am so fucked—and not in a good way. What if he's not interested?

Russ turned off the water and toweled down, resolving to take his as yet non-existent relationship with Liam one step at a time. He grabbed his lucky poker shirt—one of his favorite band tees—and headed back to the kitchen.

"Enjoy yourself?" Drew asked with a raised eyebrow.

"Shut up." Maybe Russ hadn't been as quiet as he meant to be.

"You've got it bad."

Russ opened his mouth to retort when a knock at the door saved him. Three men crowded onto the porch, each carrying a contribution of either food or alcohol for the night's entertainment.

"Is the pizza ready? I'm starving." Justin Miller shouldered his way in and dropped a box of cookies from Bear Necessities on the table. "Especially since I just flew up to Saranac and back this afternoon." The blond seaplane pilot had retrieved the missing parts for Liam's car, in between hiring out for tours and short-haul water taxi.

"I brought some Coke and the bottle of Jack I owe you from last time." Brandon Davis's tall, broad-shouldered body seemed to take up the entire kitchen. Then again, a moose shifter couldn't be expected to be a small guy. His dark eyes peered out under floppy brown hair. Brandon was a popular wilderness guide, and come summer, their game night would shift because weekends saw Brandon deep in the forest interior with his well-paying clients.

"Mom knew it was poker night, so she sent me with a fresh-baked Texas sheet cake and said to tell you to leave me gas money this time." Tyler Williams's parents owned the Fox Lake Motel, a local institution on the far end of town. Ty was a bona fide Fox Hollow native, and when he wasn't working at the hotel, he was a volunteer firefighter along with Russ, Brandon, and Justin.

"Don't bet money you can't afford to lose," Drew said, smacking Ty on the shoulder. "You're a big boy." They were all within a few years of each other in age, falling into that two-year gap between the Lowe brothers, except for Ty, who was in his late twenties.

"I got carried away," Ty replied with a grin. His tawny hair and light brown eyes were a clue to what he looked like when he was in his bobcat form, and Russ swore that's where Ty's impulsiveness came from.

Justin was the only non-shifter of the five. Anthony had proclaimed Justin to be an "honorary shifter," since he had been outnumbered. Russ's late husband had been an Apennine wolf, a variety native to Italy.

"Gimme your wallet," Russ said, rolling his eyes. He counted Ty's money, waggled the foil-wrapped condom he found for the amusement of the others, withdrew several bills, and handed them to Ty.

"There's your fun money." Russ put the wallet on top of the refrigerator. "If you try to get more out, I'll text your mom the picture of you passed out on the couch from last month's game."

Ty's eyes narrowed. "You wouldn't."

"He totally would," Drew affirmed, "and you know it."

"Fucker," Ty muttered, but his grin took the heat out of his comment.

They scarfed down the pizza, sharing whatever local gossip they'd managed to overhear or witness during the day. Fox Hollow might be small, but even when tourists weren't swelling the population, there were enough people for drama to ensue.

"…left him and took the dog, now that she found out he was getting some on the side," Brandon commented about one of their hapless acquaintances.

"Serves him right," Drew said, before he drank down the last swallow of his beer. "It's not the first time he cheated on her—she deserves better. Hell, anyone deserves better."

"Now that we've got someone new at the library, you think they'll bring back the summer theater program?" Ty asked. "My sister had her heart set on trying out, but when Walter died, everything closed down."

"Might be a good question to ask Liam," Drew said off-handedly, reaching for another bottle of beer and ignoring the stink eye Russ sent his way.

"Who's Liam?" Justin asked.

"The new librarian," Drew replied. "Russ met him when Liam had car trouble on his way into town last night."

Everyone turned to look at Russ, who managed to kick Drew none-too-gently in the shin under the table in retribution. "His car broke down. I towed him in. He said he'd just been hired. That's all I know."

"Holy shit," Justin said. "Eric Roberts is going to be pissed as hell about that."

Russ felt his wolf bristle protectively. "Why the fuck would Roberts care? He's with the Fox Institute. He doesn't have anything to do with the community—that's Jeffries."

The Fox Institute was both a part of the town life and separate from it. The Institute had courted the good graces of the town that provided them with sanctuary by participating in fundraisers for new fire trucks, recreation fields, and other needed improvements. They provided a community liaison to coordinate the programs and events at the Institute with the Fox Hollow plans for the summer arts festival and the Fall Fling, both of which brought in tourist money and garnered good-will and good PR for both parties.

But the library belonged to the town, although Jeffries sat on the oversight committee, as the Institute's representative. Chaired the committee this year, if Russ remembered correctly.

"Roberts had a nephew or some such that he wanted to see get the job," Justin replied. "One of my seaplane taxi passengers was venting on a cell phone call, and I got to hear all the ugly details. Apparently, the nephew had no relevant education or experience, but Roberts made a crack about knowing his alphabet so he could shelve books as well as anyone else."

Russ bit back a growl at the slight and Drew smirked at him.

"Roberts is a pompous ass," Ty replied, flicking a bottle cap and then fist-pumping when it landed squarely in the trash can. "He's only the Scholar-in-Residence for a year, but he acts like that means he's royalty. I don't care how many books the guy's written—he's an asshole, and everyone I've talked to can't wait for his term to be up."

"Well, Liam's got the job, moved into the bungalow, and had a tour of the place from Jeffries himself, so I'd say it's a done deal," Russ replied. "I hope Roberts isn't stupid enough to try to make trouble about it."

"Jeffries is a psychic or a medium or something, right?" Brandon asked. "Maybe he could get the ghosts to short-sheet Roberts's bed. Hide his car keys. Unscrew his toilet seat."

Russ thought all of those ideas sounded fitting, but he doubted Dr. Jeffries would enlist the aid of the dearly departed to play pranks on Roberts, no matter how well deserved.

"Hey Brandon, you hear anything else from Sheriff Armel about that hiker who went missing?" Ty asked.

Brandon shook his head and reached for another slice of pizza. "Yeah, unfortunately. Found him at the bottom of a cliff. People think just because it's a state park and there are trails that it's 'tame' somehow. There's nothing tame about these mountains."

Three days ago, they had all rallied to help search for a hiker who had failed to check back in at the ranger station. They had searched as humans and shifters, cops and first responders, taking turns. Russ and Drew weren't natives like Ty, but they knew the stories by heart about people who wandered off and were never found. A few had been children, but more were adults who vanished without a trace.

When people said the Adirondacks were "forever wild," they sometimes forgot that nature didn't play nicely.

Russ and the others took their beer and went to the table in the living room to play. None of them were on duty with the firehouse tonight, and everyone stayed over on poker night, so driving wasn't an issue, and they could all have fun.

Drew won the first game and gathered his winnings while he passed the deck to Russ to shuffle. They had long ago established an individual cap on losses at one-hundred dollars, at which point the player had to leave the game. That usually left two players pitted against each other by the end of the night, while the others watched a movie or played video games.

Russ was the first to tap out since his head wasn't in the game. He picked an action movie that everyone enjoyed seeing for the umpteenth time, and made popcorn, awaiting the next unlucky person to be banished from the game. Drew was on a roll. Ty joined Russ on the couch next and vied for control of the popcorn bowl. Justin gave up after only losing fifty dollars, bemoaning the fact that he needed maintenance on the seaplane that cut into his pocket money.

That left Brandon, and by the time the movie was over, Drew emerged the winner.

"Thank you all for a spirited set of games," Drew said, pocketing his wad of cash. Russ shot him the finger and Drew laughed. He went to the kitchen, made more popcorn, and returned with a huge bowl just as Russ started the sequel.

Everyone knew the second flick wasn't as good as the original, but by this point in the evening and the progress they'd made on the case of beer, no one cared.

The rest of the evening passed the way poker night usually went— plenty of banter, quoting dialog with favorite parts of the movies, and lots of junk food, as well as polishing off the rest of the beer.

By the time they finished the third movie, it was well after midnight. Ty had claimed the oversized armchair to sleep in, Justin watched from the comfort of the air mattress and sleeping bag he had brought, while Brandon won the rights to the couch, as the first runner-up in their games. Since Drew and Russ had their own rooms, that covered everyone.

"There's a box of doughnuts in the kitchen," Drew told them. "And I set the coffee pot to automatic brew. Just in case anyone decides to get up at an ungodly hour. I'll cook bacon when I get up—since I'm a big-hearted winner like that," he added with a grin. That got him pelted with popcorn and bottle caps, but he took a bow and danced out of the way of a new onslaught.

Since tomorrow was Sunday and tourist season hadn't started yet, that usually meant sleeping in, catching the replay of a baseball or hockey game—depending on the season—and having their company gradually drift away by noon.

Russ nursed a slight buzz and looked at the rowdy group with affection. Ty and Justin were tussling over a pillow, while Brandon carried empty bottles out to the kitchen where Drew packed up leftovers. He might have the oddest "pack," but they were all men he would trust to have his back when it counted.

Now all that's missing is your mate, his wolf added unhelpfully.

Russ said good night and ambled to his room. He made quick work of brushing his teeth and using the restroom, then stripped and set his alarm so he wouldn't miss coffee with Liam. He practically fell into bed, wiped out by the day.

He and Anthony stood on the balcony at the Adirondack Museum, looking out over the fog-wrapped blue mountains. This was a favorite place; not just for the view, but also because Anthony had proposed there. They always made a point to visit "their spot" when they came to the museum.

They stood side by side, leaning on the railing, taking in the view of autumn leaves, just as they had on their last visit before the wreck.

"It's so beautiful," Russ said. "I wish it could always stay this way."

"Everything changes," Anthony replied in the dream—which Russ knew wasn't how it had gone in real life.

"What if I don't want it to?" Dream-Russ asked.

"We don't always get a say." Anthony reached over and took his hand. Russ met his dearly-loved, deeply-missed gaze. "Sometimes, you have to let go. Spring is coming. New beginnings. That's what I want for you."

As Russ watched through teary eyes, Anthony's image faded, becoming translucent and then vanishing completely.

He woke, tears streaming down his face, heart thudding. Anthony's voice rang in his ears, far too real to have been a mere dream.

The scanner went off in the living room, sounding an alert that cut through any remaining fog of sleep. Russ ran for the scanner as Drew and the others gathered just steps behind him. He glanced at the time and saw that it was three-thirty.

"Four-alarm blaze at 423 Edgewater Road. All units report."

Ty had his phone out and was already dialing. "It's Williams. I'm with Lowe, Miller, and Davis. Do you need us to come in?"

He listened, then shook his head. "Okay. Call if you need us sooner." Ty looked up. "Chief says to come in for the morning shift, but he's covered for now."

"Shit, Edgewater Road has a bunch of seasonal homes. I wonder if anyone's even living there now?" Justin said.

"And if they aren't, then how the hell did a fire start?" Brandon asked the question that was on all of their minds.

More alcohol was out of the question now, knowing they needed to be on-duty and clear-headed in just a few hours, although Russ sorely wanted a drink, something much stiffer than beer after the dream.

"We might as well try to get a little shut-eye," Russ said, although he doubted it would work, at least for him. "Especially if we need to relieve the night shift."

Everyone headed back to their places, and Russ closed his door behind him and debated whether to sit up in the reading chair for the rest of the night. The bed he had shared with Anthony had been a source of comfort, and at his worst moments, he had almost been able to imagine his husband's embrace when he was wrapped tightly in sheets and blankets. He had purchased a new bed last year but had never shared it with anyone.

Now his heart felt torn and confused. Sensing Anthony's presence at the cemetery, dreaming of him just moments ago still consoled Russ. But as much as it confounded him, he could not deny the reality of the connection he felt to Liam, something he never expected to experience.

At least to Russ's way of reckoning, Anthony had made it clear that he did not oppose Russ finding his fated mate. That eased his guilt over the undeniable magnetism that drew him to Liam. But his own reaction was only half the equation.

What if Liam doesn't want to take a chance?

Russ didn't have an answer to that. *Shit. I've got to go into the firehouse first thing. That means I'm going to have to cancel my first "date" with Liam. Fuck. That is not going to get us off on the right footing.*

He crawled back into bed and managed to drift off, but it seemed like only moments passed before the alarm went off, starting a day that felt likely to pose more questions than answers.

3

LIAM

Liam's first full day in Fox Hollow started remarkably well. Even though it was Saturday, he woke without an alarm at eight in the morning. Liam felt disoriented in a strange place until memories caught up with him, and he realized he was *home*. That big shift was going to take some getting used to.

Coffee and doughnuts in the kitchen reminded him of the kindness of strangers, and he sank into a chair cradling a hot cup of java and staring into its inky surface as if it might reveal the mysteries of the universe.

Just yesterday, a Huntsman had tried to kill him.

Yesterday, he learned that his ex-boyfriend turned him over to a hitman for a bounty.

Less than twenty-four hours ago, he fled his job and apartment and everyone he knew to stay one step ahead of a killer.

Then he ran for his life, broke down by the side of the road, and very possibly met his fated mate.

And now he had a new home and a different job, in a town he'd never visited before.

Liam took a couple of slow, deep breaths and tried not to pass out.

Over the course of his life, more than one person had accused him of being "dramatic"—never in a good way. Liam owned that some of that went with his birth sign of Leo, and even more with being a fox shifter. Now, he just wished he could show those condescending mofos that this was him *not being dramatic* in light of circumstances that would probably push anyone sane over the edge.

Liam gripped the cup hard enough that he worried it might break. *How did I end up with this shitshow for a life? I've always played it fairly safe, especially for a Leo. Stayed in school. Got a graduate degree. I'm a fucking librarian, for God's sake!*

Did I join the Foreign Legion? No!

Did I backpack solo across battle zones carrying only a toothbrush and a change of underwear? No!

Didn't rob a bank, or rat out the Mob, or piss off a cartel.

So remind me again how I ended up with a hitman after my ass?

Oh, yeah. Rotten taste in boyfriends.

Liam's hands were shaking. He'd "gotten his dander up" as his mother used to say. Maybe he was being a little dramatic after all.

But his mother was dead from cancer, his father had long ago skipped town after deciding that a shifter wife and son were too weird for his taste, and there hadn't been any other family to speak of, nothing that counted as a true skulk, the fox equivalent of a pack.

He had once thought Kelson might be family enough.

Obviously not.

Why had Kelson turned him over to a Huntsman? Normal people broke up with partners every day without hiring a hitman to kidnap their former boyfriend and turn him over to wealthy sadistic trophy hunters to track and kill for sport. Apparently shifter trafficking was a lucrative black market—but hardly something Liam could have gone to the cops about.

He ran a hand through his hair, not feeling rested at all though he had dropped into an exhausted sleep as soon as his head hit the pillow.

The breakup with Kelson hadn't even been recent. They'd broken up six months ago, long enough that Liam had started to heal, at least on the outside. Learning to trust again after Kelson's cheating would take time. And after having a fucking price put on his head for his pelt?

Liam didn't know how to begin to get over that.

So why was his first waking thought about Russ?

Just thinking the hunky wolf shifter's name brought Russ's scent to mind, and Liam's traitorous cock obviously hadn't gotten the message about swearing off men.

Last night, Liam had been losing his shit, stranded on the side of the road. Then Russ had come to his rescue, and everything about the man promised safety, protection, security, nurturing. He'd listened, shown kindness, and gone out of his way for Liam. And while Liam felt certain Russ would have done the same for anyone, he couldn't deny the crackle of psychic electricity that had arced through his heart and soul when their fingers touched.

Liam had never believed in fated mates. Sure, he'd read the romance books and enjoyed the stories. But if such a thing did exist, Liam had convinced himself it was for other types of shifters—wolves, bears, big cats.

Did foxes have fated mates? And if they did, could a fox and a wolf possibly be soulmates?

Being a librarian meant knowing how to research. Liam decided he had a new project—to find out everything he could about fated mates.

With a groan, Liam put down his empty mug, staggered to the shower, and tried to clear his head.

He hadn't just awakened to thoughts of Russ. He'd woken with a stiff, aching cock from a wet dream so vivid he'd creamed his sleep pants like a teenager.

Russ's muscles looked even better naked. His solid body pinned Liam to the mattress just the way he liked it, and the bristle of his salt-and-pepper body hair against Liam's smooth skin made every nerve tingle.

Strong thighs and a sculpted ass had Liam hard and dripping even before he'd gotten a glimpse of Russ's thick, uncut cock and heavy balls.

All the better to fuck you with, my dear.

Liam knew he looked like a twink, but he was more than capable of topping, and he liked to switch. With a guy Russ's size, the idea of taking it up against the wall sounded like something out of his favorite porn. But Dream-Russ moved slowly and carefully, not like he thought Liam was fragile, but because he thought he was precious. Valuable. Worthy of savoring.

Even when Liam had begged, the Russ in his dream took his time, a careful and generous lover, making sure Liam's needs were met beyond his wildest expectations. Then Russ had chased his own release, shooting deep inside Liam's ass, bareback so Liam felt his hot come marking him, filling him up. Liam had tilted his head, baring his neck, an unspoken invitation.

Russ had growled, and then his teeth pierced the skin, claiming Liam as his own —

"Holy shit, that was hot," Liam muttered, unable to avoid noticing that he was already hard again, just from the memory.

My brain needed some good chemicals, and whipped up a perfect lover with Russ's face and body, Liam told himself. *Shit, I bet I could count on both hands how many times I've jerked off since Kelson and I broke up. Wasn't in the mood. Now I meet Mr. Sexy Wolf, and I'm hot and ready?*

I've got to get a grip. I think I'm losing my mind.

His fox swished its red, bushy tail, impatiently. *No, we've found our mate.*

Fated mates are only in romance books.

Amber eyes narrowed, unamused. *He is our mate. His scent is unmistakable. Not like that other one.*

Liam sighed. *I was wrong not to listen to you.*

That tail swish could have outdone the flick of a feather boa from every drag queen on every runway in the world. *I tried to tell you, darling. You wouldn't listen. But what do I know? I'm only your wildly intuitive other half.*

Dramatic much?

The fox smiled at him, baring the tips of his fangs and a bit of his pink tongue. *Always. Might as well add cunning and wily—we're going to need it with a huntsman after this beautiful tail.*

No one is getting your tail.

Maybe not mine, but you can give yours up to that gorgeous wolf any time, his fox replied, with an expression Liam could only consider a leer. *He might be a wolf, but he's a total silver fox.*

Liam sighed in exasperation. *He's only a few years older than I am. Ever heard of premature gray?*

Or as I call it, "hello, Daddy."

You're incorrigible.

Oh sweetie, I encourage a lot. We could do worse than having a wolf watching our back. No one is going to come through him to get to us. We'd be safe.

Liam cringed, admitting that the same calculation had crossed his very-human mind. *Russ is a good guy. I'm not going to use him for protection. I don't want anyone to get hurt.*

I deserve to be a kept fox. I have expensive tastes. Raw rabbit disturbs my digestion.

I am not looking to be a "kept" anything. Give me a little breathing room. I need to figure things out.

That tail swished again, eloquent without words. *Fated matings are never wrong. You picked the last few boyfriends, and how did that work out? But what do I know...*

With that, his fox flounced off to the corners of his mind, but the glint in his amber eyes made it clear he relished having the last word.

The very cool shower left Liam shivery, but it dissuaded his over-eager cock from going for round two. Liam finished dressing, and checked the time, realizing he still had quite a while before Dr. Jeffries came to show him around town.

I should go check on the car. Things were crazy last night. I might have left something out or written it down wrong. And it wouldn't hurt to thank Russ again for saving my ass. Just checking on the Honda.

Mmmm-hmm. His fox sounded smug.

Liam forced himself not to think about all the other, very pleasant things his awakening libido wanted to check on, like those salacious details of his morning wood jerk off session.

If he was truly honest with himself, he saw signs that things were going wrong with Kelson long before they split up. He'd met Kelson in graduate school when Liam had been alone and vulnerable. His mother had just died, and while his small inheritance plus his scholarships got him through Ithaca, what he had in drive and intelligence made up for what he lacked at that time in confidence, "drama fox" notwithstanding.

Kelson had seemed so sure of himself, worldly-wise, capable, and strong. Liam had just wanted a shelter from the storm, a place he could lay his burdens down, someone to hold him through the nights and help him piece his world back together after his mother's passing.

It took a couple of years, given the distractions of pressing deadlines and defending his thesis, to realize that Kelson talked a better game than he delivered. He had endless advice on how Liam could do everything better, but turned a blind eye to his own areas for development. Kelson could flatter and ingratiate when he wanted something—like Liam's body—but his responses were much less enthusiastic when Liam was the one in need.

In the end, he'd just been one more entitled trust fund baby. The fact that he was all-human, like Liam's deadbeat dad, now seemed like a warning sign Liam had ignored at his own risk.

Yeah, #NotAllHumans. I get it. And there are human-shifter couples out there who make it work somehow. But if I ever fall in love again—and that's a helluva big "if"—I want a honey with a side of fur.

Oh…kinky, his fox purred.

Shut up.

I'll be in my bunk.

Liam sighed and rolled his eyes, although no one was there to see him. He guzzled another cup of coffee, promised himself a run in his fur later to sort things out with his well-meaning but annoying diva-fox, and shouldered into his coat for the trip across the street to check on Russ. *I mean, on my car. Totally meant the car.*

A pleasant young woman with red hair and bright blue eyes looked up when he entered. "I'm Liam Reynard," he told her. "Russ towed my car last night, and I wanted to stop in and see if he needed anything else from me."

Oh God, that sounds so wrong.

"I mean, if there was any missing information," Liam hastened to clarify. "It was late and things were kinda crazy."

"I'm Kerrie," she said with a smile. "And I don't know if there's anything else, but I'll ask."

His conversation with Russ was short, sweet, and awkward. When Liam found himself back on the sidewalk, the time had passed in a blur, but the smell of grease, gasoline, and coffee mingled with Russ's scent calmed him, smoothing over the morning's rough spots.

Liam had never been so eager to stop back at a garage later in the day.

He hurried home, just in time to greet Dr. Jeffries.

"I come bearing gifts," his mentor said, holding out a homemade coffee cake.

"Thank you so much." Liam accepted the cake, inhaling the smell of cinnamon and nutmeg. "Would you like a slice and some coffee? The pot is still hot."

"How about instead, I introduce you to the place where I bought both your coffee and the cake?" Jeffries said. "Bear Necessities—local place, best you'll ever taste."

"I am all for that."

"Then let's go take a tour of the library, and we'll head to the Bear for lunch before you get the grand walking tour of Fox Hollow," Jeffries said with a grin.

"This keyring has everything you need for the building," Jeffries said as they walked around to the front door of the library, which was a solid three-story rectangular brick building with neat but minimal landscaping.

"The keys are color-coded—you'll catch on. Front door, back door, your office, the maintenance room, the receptionist's desk drawers, the rare book room, the attic."

"There's a rare book room?" Despite everything, Liam felt a thrill of excitement.

Jeffries chuckled. "Probably not as big as some, but it has local journals, letters, photographs…things that are important to the folks here."

Two women looked up when they entered. "Liam, I'd like you to meet Linda and Maddi, the two most dedicated and wonderful volunteers in the world," Jeffries said. Liam didn't have any question about which name went with which person. "Ladies, this is Liam Reynard, the new head librarian."

Liam stepped forward to shake their hands. He guessed that Linda might be in her early sixties, with short dark hair and mocha skin, average height, and a solid, compact build. His fox roused when they shook hands, tail twitching.

She's some kind of dog. Basset hound? Beagle? Could be a good ally.

Maddi was probably in her late teens, with brown hair pulled up in a ponytail and expressive blue eyes. She was petite and even shorter than Liam. He couldn't help smiling back at her broad grin and noticed that she seemed to be almost bouncing with energy.

She's a shifter, but I'm not sure what. Some kind of cat. Also a good ally.

Liam wondered what his two new acquaintances made of him, and whether they read his "other half" just as easily. If so, no one commented.

"I was just giving Liam the grand tour," Jeffries told them. "Linda and Maddi do pretty much everything around here—pull and re-shelve books, handle interlibrary loans, manage new media orders, oversee the lending program, and a lot more. But they really shine with the community programs, the festivals, and the arts outreach."

He clapped Liam on the shoulder. "They get to do the fun stuff, which leaves you more time to fill out paperwork, handle the budget, be the liaison to the city council, the Institute, and the festival planning committees."

Liam smiled. "I'm looking forward to all of that," he replied, and he meant it. No one liked paperwork, although Liam knew it went with the job. But his fox excelled in anything that smacked of a "performance," which included presentations and committee meetings. Foxes had a reputation for clever maneuvering that was well-deserved. His Leo nature just put that into overdrive.

"Welcome," Linda said. "Enjoy the tour. I'll bring in muffins on Monday and maybe we can sit down over coffee and talk about some of the plans for the summer. It's going to be here before we know it!"

"That sounds fantastic," Liam said. "I'm all ears, and I do have some ideas that worked well at my old library, so maybe we can figure out if they'd add anything here as well."

Linda elbowed Jeffries. "New blood. This is going to be fun." She looked to Liam. "I worked with Walter here at the library for ten years, and Maddi's been with us since she was in middle school. Walter did a great job and believed in the power of a good book. But he wasn't well at the end, and some things got put on the back burner."

Maddi rolled her eyes. "What she's also saying is that you're a lot younger, so that bodes well for technology, new ideas, and internet stuff. We all loved Walter, but let's just say he wasn't a huge fan of computers."

Liam laughed. "Fair enough. I can't wait to put our heads together."

With a wave and a promise to bring back lattes for the two volunteers, Liam followed Jeffries into the next room. He knew a small-town library would be dwarfed by the big university counterparts he'd grown used to. But he realized the real difference in size when he noticed that the main circulating collection here could have probably fit into two good-sized rooms in a normal house.

"Don't judge a book by the size of its cover," Jeffries joked. "Walter and Linda did a great job of curating the catalog to offer a wide range of materials, while also going deep on favorites like mysteries, thrillers, and romance. We have a busy interlibrary loan program too. Ebooks and audiobooks as well. And for being up in years, Walter had a progressive streak, so there are all kinds of books for LGBTQ youth, mental health topics, and more. I doubt there's a dusty book on the shelves."

Liam nodded, understanding what Jeffries meant. A big collection that was either outdated or not in sync with local tastes might look impressive but didn't do anyone much good. He'd much rather need to replace a copy because the binding was falling off from overuse than have pristine tomes no one ever bothered to borrow.

"That was the main room," Jeffries said, beckoning for Liam to follow him.

"There's a computer to search the catalog at the main desk and a self-service one over there," Jeffries went on, pointing to a kiosk. "This is the public computer area," he added, walking into a small, narrow room off to one side that held two old desktop computers. "All grant funded. We can talk about the details later." He didn't slow down, but Liam silently made a list of things to discuss with Linda and Maddi.

"Then this is the reference area," Jeffries said, heading into a smaller room with two big desks and lots of familiar dictionaries, how-to manuals, cookbooks, and study materials. "And here's the rare book area."

Liam eagerly followed him into a room that might have been the size of a generous walk-in closet, with walls lined floor-to-ceiling with old leather-bound volumes and a flat storage unit for what Liam guessed were maps, artwork, and blueprints.

"The rare book room receives an annual bequest, as does the children's area," Jeffries said. "Linda can give you the basics, and then you and I can talk later when we go over the budget, allocations, and politics."

They headed upstairs, where Jeffries showed off a brightly painted and recently re-carpeted children's area that looked well-stocked and friendly, as well as a community room that could hold a good crowd.

"The attic is a climate-controlled third floor for storage. All the usual maintenance stuff is in the basement. Given the weather here, there's good heat but no AC. Plenty of fans up in the attic that can be brought down if you need them," he added. "There's also a staff room off the community area with a shared kitchenette."

"I'm impressed," Liam said. "This is a lot for a small town. That suggests that there are plenty of readers, some generous donors, and years of good oversight."

Jeffries smiled, obviously pleased at Liam's sincere praise.

"Fox Hollow isn't a big place, but people here do their best for each other. That's one of the things I've liked about moving here," Jeffries said as they waved goodbye to Linda and Maddi and headed down the front steps toward the street.

Last night Liam hadn't gotten a good look at the town, and this morning when he'd run to the auto shop, he was so focused on getting back in time to meet Jeffries that he didn't pause to take in the scenery.

Now, he stopped when they reached the sidewalk and took in his surroundings. Across the street on his right was a clothing shop, a large gift and bookstore, and the Unitarian church, which looked like it had a cemetery behind it, and a stretch of woods beyond that. To the left of the library was the police station, sheriff's office, and fire department, housed in one building, with a grocery store at the bend in the road.

"Don't know if you did any scouting this morning," Jeffries said as they fell into step together, "but behind the library are the schools, ballfields, community building, the medical center, and of course, Fox Institute."

"Fox Hollow reminds me of the library," Liam said, feeling like a tourist as he looked from side to side. "Lots of good stuff in a small package."

Jeffries chuckled. "I'd say you're right on target. If you want something unusual, you might have to go to one of the bigger towns or buy online. But the town council and the local chamber have worked hard to assure that the services and stores in town provide the residents as well as the tourists with everything they need ninety-nine percent of the time."

Liam had feared regular trips to stock up might be the penalty for small-town living, and with his car on the fritz, that had worried him. He felt his shoulders loosen a little with at least one source of concern put to rest.

"Everything looks well-cared for," he observed. "That usually means people are doing pretty well for themselves."

Jeffries shrugged. "We like to think so. Some businesses are seasonal because of the weather or the tourists—or both. But those folks have a side gig for the other part of the year. The Institute also brings in people all year round, including for the Winter Retreat, when the only other outsiders we get are for the snowmobile rally."

Just past the bend in the road, Liam saw Bear Necessities Coffee and Café, with a big painted cutout of a black bear holding the day's chalkboard menu. He realized it was right across the street from Russ's car care complex, a detail he had completely missed in the craziness of the previous night.

"Let's get some coffee and a sandwich, I'll answer any of your questions, and then I want to make sure we at least walk as far as the big hotel and the beach. It's worth it," Jeffries promised.

The coffee shop had forest green clapboard siding, with red trim on the shutters and door. Most of the buildings that Liam had seen so far were wooden and looked to be repurposed from previous uses, which gave the town a sense of history and preserved ties to its past.

"Hi, Sherri," Jeffries greeted the woman behind the counter.

Sherri flicked a loose strand of brown hair out of her eyes and smiled broadly. "Hey there, Rich. Who's your friend?"

"This is Liam Reynard, the new head librarian," Jeffries replied. "I've been bragging to him about your coffee and sandwiches, so I figured I'd better bring him here to find out for himself."

"You have come to the right place," Sherri told Liam, leaning over the counter as if imparting a secret. "There's no better coffee in these mountains between here and Canada."

Sherri's smile lit up the room. She had an ample, curvy build that reminded Liam of a classical Greek statue. "Tell me what you want— choices are up on the board; Rich can give you his opinions—and then get a table and we'll bring it out to you."

They discussed the combinations and placed their orders, then Liam followed Jeffries to a table off to one side, where they could speak with a degree of privacy.

"Sherri and Nelson are the cousins of Torben Armel, the town sheriff," Jeffries said. "Bear shifters."

"With the Institute and the shifters, how much of the town…isn't?"

Jeffries chuckled. "If I had to guess, I'd say about a quarter aren't either psychic or a shifter. But those folks are usually here because there's still a tie to the supernatural. They might be witches, Wiccan, pagan—the Old Ways. Or they're married to someone who is a paranormal, or have a family member who is."

He dropped his voice. "We love to have visitors. But we try hard to make sure Fox Hollow remains a sanctuary for the people who need it, so we don't encourage relocation as a general rule."

Liam raised an eyebrow." What made you take a chance on me?"

"I knew you'd fit in here," Jeffries said with a shrug. "Fox Hollow is a place for people who need a home. The legends around how the town got founded say that it was started by a pair of shifters who were best friends but were different types of animals. For that, they were exiled from their homes. They came here and made a camp. Little by little, other misfit shifters found their way to Fox Hollow, predators and prey animals, carnivores, omnivores, and herbivores. All different —except for the one thing they had in common: that they didn't fit in with their own kind."

Jeffries grinned. "We have one strict rule in Fox Hollow—don't eat your neighbors. So I don't think you'll have any trouble feeling at home here." He sighed. "And I had a premonition that you were going to need a place to go."

Liam met the man's gaze, trying to guess how much the psychic knew. His admission confirmed Liam's suspicion that the well-timed offer hadn't been a coincidence.

"I appreciate that," he said, knowing that he should come clean with Jeffries about the Huntsman, but unwilling to do so in a public place.

I'll tell him later. I need to go sign papers. That'll be a good time.

Jeffries filled him in on the town's many events, as well as what to expect in tourist season. Liam listened intently and asked plenty of questions, already coming up with new ideas for the library to engage visitors around the themes of reading and art.

"What about hunting season?" Liam asked. "That's got to be a danger."

Jeffries nodded. "Between the Institute and some of the town's old founding families, there's a fifty-mile radius of privately-owned land that surrounds the town and is posted *'No Hunting or Trapping.'* No birds or mammals may be harmed, although fishing is permitted."

Another of Liam's concerns melted away. He was just about to ask another question when Sherri bustled up with a tray.

"Reuben on house-made rye with a house-made pickle and small-batch kettle chips," she said, setting a plate in front of Liam. "And to answer your question from up front—yes, the PBBJ sandwich is amazing. Peanut butter, banana, and jelly, we grind our own nut butter, and the jellies and jams are locally made."

Liam gave a moan of joy. "That makes me so happy. Other sandwiches can be phenomenal, but nothing compares to an awesome PB&J. It's the most perfect combination in the universe."

Sherri and Jeffries chuckled at his enthusiastic reaction. "Well aren't you the sweetest thing?" Sherri clucked. "Tell you what, next time, try the PBBJ and let me know what you think."

Liam blushed, while his fox preened. "Sorry, I get rather…passionate…about things I like."

"You don't have to apologize to me," Sherri said, making a show of fanning herself. "I haven't heard anyone get that hot and bothered since my knitting circle all went to see that Jason Momoa merman movie. If you still feel the same way after you eat one of the sandwiches, we might just put you on the website for a testimonial. Maybe we'll rename the sandwich, call it the Bust-a-Nut."

"Sherri! Are you harassing that nice man?" Nelson called from behind the counter, but his wide grin assured Liam he was joking.

"Never, sweetie. You're all the bear I'll ever need," Sherri replied. She turned back to the table and finished unloading her tray. "Southwest chicken on ciabatta with local pepper-jack cheese, house-made aioli, and hand-cut potato wedges," Sherri added, setting down Jeffries's plate. Two tall glasses of ice water accompanied their order and a plate with a pair of giant chocolate-chip cookies.

"Cookies are on the house. Welcome to Fox Hollow. We're glad you're here," she said with a wink and a grin directed at Liam.

They dug into the food, and Liam realized he was hungrier than he thought. Halfway through their meal, a thin, balding man in a tweed jacket stalked up to their table. He gave Liam a dismissive once-over and turned to Jeffries, who had stiffened with an unreadable expression on his face.

"This is your pick? Hardly a seasoned professional."

"This is not the place, Eric," Jeffries said in a low voice, with an unmistakable edge of warning. "We can discuss this in my office—but the matter is closed."

"I'll lodge a complaint," the newcomer threatened.

Jeffries didn't look worried. "You are free to do that, but it won't change anything."

"We'll see about that." The stranger walked off, and Liam noticed that Sherri paid attention as the man left. She glanced over to Jeffries, who shrugged and shook his head. Liam felt sure from her expression that the man was not one of her favorites.

"I'm sorry about that," Jeffries said, drawing Liam's attention once more. "Eric Roberts is a temporary faculty member at the Institute. He put a candidate forward for the librarian position. The committee chose you instead."

Liam had a million questions, but he knew Jeffries wouldn't be permitted to answer any of them, so he just smiled and nodded, and went back to his food. Jeffries looked annoyed and embarrassed by Roberts's display, but Liam didn't sense that his companion thought the man was dangerous. He had no desire to plunge into small-town politics on his first day, so he was happy to let the incident pass.

As they finished their lunch, Liam and Jeffries chatted about mutual acquaintances from Ithaca, compared the weather there to Fox Hollow, and talked about the essentials Liam would need for a much harsher winter than he had ever experienced.

By the time they finished eating, Liam felt happily stuffed. The coffee and sandwich were as good as Jeffries had claimed, and the cookies were among the best he'd ever had. Liam knew he'd quickly become a regular.

They thanked Sherri for the cookies as they settled the bill, which Jeffries insisted on paying as part of Liam's "welcome tour."

"Don't be a stranger," Sherri told Liam, handing him a coffee rewards card.

"Let's walk down to the beach, and then we can pick up the lattes we promised Linda and Maddi on the way back to my office. I need you to sign some paperwork, and I can at least give you a glimpse of the Institute while you're there."

They passed an antique shop whose windows were full of pieces Liam could only term "rustic-chic." Next door was a camping and fishing outfitter, and beside it was the office for seaplane tours and water taxi service, with a plane bobbing on the lake at the end of the dock.

"Wow." Liam looked out over Fox Lake, taking in the blue water, tree-lined shores, and the rocky outcroppings that jutted into the lapping waves. Then he turned and saw the large white Victorian hotel on the other side of the road.

"That's why I wanted to bring you down here," Jeffries said, grinning. "To see our two biggest treasures—the lake, and the Fox Hollow Hotel."

"It's beautiful." Part of what drew Liam to books and libraries was his love of history, and the old hotel intrigued him.

"It's even prettier on the inside," Jeffries said with pride. "The locals usually go to the bar, and in the summer, the deck has drinks and entertainment. But the inside is all rustic Victorian, and so it's the place to go for weddings, parties, and special celebrations. Food's good too."

The more Liam saw of his new town, the more he felt at peace with his panicked and impetuous decision to relocate. *And if hunting is forbidden, that's got to make it at least a little difficult for the Huntsman to track me here. I hope.*

"There's more," Jeffries said with a shrug as if he had admitted to an embarrassment of riches. "Down that way is the Seneca Theater— another Victorian gem—for both movies and live performances. And scattered around, we've got a surprising number of good places to eat because up here, we move on our stomachs." He underscored his words by patting his belly.

"I'm going to have a good time exploring," Liam said, feeling excited about the possibilities. A flicker of hope stirred, no longer smothered by fear. Maybe he would be safe here, and with luck, be among friends.

Safer with a wolf for a mate, his fox reminded him.

"I should go pick up my car," Liam said, glancing at a new message on his phone and then eyeing Russ's auto shop. "Can I meet up with you at the library?"

Jeffries nodded. "Sure. I'll pick up the lattes and meet you there."

Liam felt slightly horrified to realize he was *giddy* over retrieving his car from the garage. His fox preened, flicking his very handsome, full tail, nearly prancing—posturing to attract a mate.

Quit that, Liam admonished.

I just want to be ready for our yummy wolf.

He isn't "our" wolf.

Fated mate, darling. He most definitely is ours—and decidedly delicious.

Liam pushed his fox back and headed to the garage, where Russ quickly came out to speak with him. When Russ mentioned having parts flown in to speed up the work, and throwing in a free tune-up, Liam had to admit his fox might be right about Russ being equally smitten. And when Russ invited him for coffee tomorrow, Liam couldn't deny that his heart skipped a beat, even though his mind still protested *too much, too fast, too dangerous.*

Just catching a whiff of Russ's scent—heightened by sweat and a touch of grease—chubbed Liam up like a horny teenager. He could easily lose himself in those green eyes, and from the way Russ's pupils looked blown wider than usual, he sensed that the other man felt the same magnetism.

He'd always laughed about the idea of "sexual tension" in books and movies, but whatever was between the two of them was real and thick enough to cut with a knife.

His thoughts were still whirling when he drove away, parking in a spot near the bungalow. Jeffries was waiting for him at the library reception desk, where Maddi had desk duty.

"Everything okay with the car?" Jeffries asked.

Liam nodded. "Done early, with a tune-up thrown in." He chose to ignore Jeffries's raised eyebrow. "Ready to go to the Institute?"

Maddi assured them she and Linda would lock up, and Liam wished them a quiet Sunday, with a promise to see them for brainstorming on Monday.

The walk to the Fox Institute took them past the schools and recreation area, as well as several professional buildings. Nestled against the backdrop of tall pines sat another large Victorian structure, easily the same size as the hotel.

"That's the original school and dormitory the refugees from Lily Dale built," Jeffries said with pride. "They brought whatever wealth they could carry with them, and had this completed within a year."

He pointed to newer buildings nearby. "Over time, the art center got its own building, and the dormitories too. The senior center and community college aren't directly related to the Institute, but there's a long history of providing programs and resources."

"So the community and the Institute get along?"

Jeffries nodded. "Most of the time. We need each other, and we're safer together."

"Is everyone here a psychic?" Liam asked as they walked up the broad front steps.

"Psychic, medium, clairvoyant—all the abilities most people don't believe are real. Some people can channel spirits, others get glimpses of the future." Jeffries looked around as if seeing things with a fresh eye.

"The group from Lily Dale started with a few cabins that first winter. The shifters and other paranormals in Fox Hollow helped them get settled. Of course, the Spiritualists wanted to continue their research and their efforts to learn more about the unseen world. They made sure to get off on a good footing with the shifters, witches, and others, and assure that they didn't mean any harm."

"So everyone...gets along?" Liam asked.

Jeffries shrugged. "Better than in most places. I guess we all remember that we weren't welcome where we were 'supposed' to fit in, so we're maybe a little more grateful for our own little misfit community."

Liam took that in and thought about it for a moment. "Let's go back to the psychic thing. That's what you do? See things you couldn't know any other way?"

"It's a skill I didn't understand for a long time," Jeffries replied, leading Liam up a mahogany staircase and down a hallway to his office, which must have once been one of the dormitory rooms. From what Liam saw of the common areas, the Institute had an atmosphere of restrained elegance. The disgraced spiritualists might have fled hardship, but they had not gone into the wilderness without resources.

Liam found that oddly comforting, having just made a similar journey. He hoped it worked out for him as well as it had for them.

"Please, sit down. I have your papers here," Jeffries said, motioning Liam to a chair in front of his desk as he reached for a folder.

"This should be everything," he said, setting out the folder and a pen.

Liam scanned the forms, forcing himself to pay attention and read them closely. He tapped the pen nervously as he read.

Should I tell him about the Huntsman now? What if it makes him change his mind? But if I don't tell him and it brings harm to the town, I'll have lost everything anyhow, and caused others to be hurt.

I have to say something.

Just as Liam took a breath to speak, the door to the office slammed open, and Eric Roberts strode in without bothering to knock.

"How dare you! You hired your favorite without even bothering to interview the other candidates." The man's features were twisted with rage.

Jeffries rose and walked around the desk to put himself between Liam and the newcomer.

"You're out of line, Roberts," Jeffries snapped in a cold tone Liam had never heard his mentor use before. "Get out of my office."

"I put in a candidate for consideration. You had no right—"

"You submitted a candidate that lacked the necessary education or credentials," Jeffries replied, biting off every word. "He had no experience, no references, nothing to even indicate an interest in the position. All you wanted was a job for your nephew. Things don't work like this here, even if you are the year's Scholar."

Roberts vibrated with anger. "You have no right!"

"I have every right. The hiring went through proper channels. The candidate had all of the necessary requirements as well as additional skills. It's over. The job has been filled. Leave before you embarrass yourself further," Jeffries ordered.

"Or what?" Roberts demanded.

Jeffries took another step toward the intruder. "Or I will see what secrets I can find by rummaging through your brain. I had my doubts about your suitability to be Scholar-in-Residence, which were ignored by the selection committee. I let it drop to keep the peace. You do not want me for an enemy. Now get out—and if you make trouble about this, I will ferret out whatever it is you do not want revealed."

Roberts paled, although his jaw remained clenched in fury. He cast a disparaging look at Liam, then turned on his heel and strode out, slamming the door behind him.

Liam gripped the arms of the chair, ready to spring into action to defend Jeffries or himself.

"Relax," Jeffries said, managing a smile, although Liam could see the strain in his features. "I'll handle Roberts. He's only here for a year —more of a novelty than a real part of the faculty. He wrote a couple of books and thinks he knows everything."

"Can you do that? What you told him you would do?" Liam asked, in a voice barely above a whisper.

Jeffries shrugged. "If I truly needed to. Hardly worth the effort for someone like him." He perched on the edge of the desk, facing Liam. "Don't let him bother you. No one listens to him—that's part of what got him riled up in the first place. Everyone's excited to have you here."

Liam nodded, swallowing hard. *He stuck his neck out for me. If I tell him now, he might regret his choice. Maybe the Huntsman won't track me. Maybe he'll find an easier target. If I think he's found me, I'll say something then.*

Liam finished signing the papers and handed the folder back to Jeffries. "Thank you. I promise I'll do my best."

Jeffries laid a hand on his shoulder. "I know you will. That's why I supported you as a candidate. You're also a shifter, which is good for the community."

Liam startled because he hadn't confided that secret to his old mentor. *He's psychic—remember?*

"Fox Hollow is a place of sanctuary. We watch out for our own." The intensity of the look Jeffries gave him made Liam wonder if the other man already suspected—or knew—the truth about the Huntsman.

Liam dropped his gaze, feeling too exposed. "Thank you. I won't let you down."

"That possibility never crossed my mind," Jeffries replied, relaxing enough to smile. "Monday, I'll come by the library after lunch, and we can go over budgets and all that fun stuff. Enjoy tomorrow and go exploring."

Liam half expected to find Roberts waiting for him in the corridor, but to his relief, he didn't catch a glimpse of the angry man. Still rattled, Liam tried to let the cool breeze and the waning afternoon sun clear his mood.

We need to run, his fox told him, pacing in his mind. *Let me out.*

For once, Liam agreed whole-heartedly.

Everything he had seen today made him feel sure he was going to like it here. And despite his misgivings and his vow to avoid "man trouble," Liam had to admit that Russ challenged his resolve.

Liam wasn't ready to trot through town in his fur just yet, so he decided he would walk over to the woods behind the cemetery across the street, find a place to stash his clothing and shift, and then have a nice run before it got too late. The sun was low in the sky, late afternoon but not yet twilight, and while it was a bit early for his fox, Liam didn't feel comfortable enough to go exploring after dark.

He cut through the parking lot behind the church, then walked quickly along the edge of the trees, looking for a good place to hide his clothing. He found a large tree not far inside the edge of the woods, in a spot he felt certain he could find again.

Spring in the Adirondacks didn't lend itself to outdoor nudity for a lot of reasons, which began with the temperature and moved right on to deer flies. Fortunately, Liam shifted quickly, so the discomfort and risk of frostbite and insect bites was minimal. He just had to concentrate to make the change, something that seemed as natural as breathing.

It felt good to be back in his fur. Several days had passed since the last time Liam shifted, and it reminded him how important it was to keep both sides of his nature in balance.

You know you need me. I'm too fabulous to ignore, his fox snarked.

Humble fellow, aren't you?

Never. Why hide it when you've got it?

Liam just shook his head and trotted off, reveling in how sharp his senses were like this. Sight, sound, smell all took on an entirely new dimension, coupled with fox speed and agility. Liam could feel the earth's magnetic field coursing beneath everything, imparting a sense of direction, telling him where to find prey and how to judge distance.

His whiskers quivered, reading the air around him, alert for food or danger. Liam couldn't pick up the scent-marking of any other foxes, which meant no one was likely to pose a challenge to the territory. At some point, he'd go looking for the "real" foxes, get to know *all* the neighbors. But for now, he just wanted to shake off his cares and lose himself in a good run.

Liam sprinted, feeling his heart pound and his breath quicken. He pounced a few times at piles of leaves just for the sport of it, not intending to actually catch the mouse or chipmunk hiding beneath. He rolled on the ground, breathing in the loamy smell, listening to the wind in the trees and the song of the birds.

Joy. That was the only word Liam could find for this overwhelming feeling. He hoped that someday, he might feel it just as strongly as a man as he did as a fox.

Maybe someday.

Liam darted among the trees, nearly drunk on the heady smell of balsam. His runs back in Ithaca had been short and careful, limited to a few parks where he felt safe. He hadn't known to fear Kelson, but he did have a healthy respect for Animal Control and had no desire to wind up on the wrong end of a dogcatcher's pole.

His human side couldn't help being intrigued by the cemetery behind the weathered stone church. This was the old section, with stones and monuments clearly dating back to the middle of the eighteen-hundreds. Liam vowed to come back in his skin to read the inscriptions. Maybe he could find someone steeped in local history to show him around and tell him stories. Wandering old graveyards was a passion, one he had not indulged in a long time.

Do shifters bury their dead here? Or does it vary by the type? Liam's mother had no skulk of her own, and so when she passed, he had mourned her in human fashion. He'd known only a few shifters and none of them well enough to pick their brains about shifter etiquette. What little he found online hadn't always been accurate. Maybe now that he was in Fox Hollow, he could embrace his full shifter heritage, without fear or shame.

I bet our wolf could teach us a lot of new tricks, his fox said with a smirk.

Liam chose to ignore his other side and trotted along the edge of the woods, crossing over from the older section directly behind the church to the more recent gravesites in an adjacent plot.

New markers just don't have the same style and artistry, Liam thought. *The old stones seem more personal, less slick.*

Liam caught Russ's scent before he spotted the man striding through the new section of the cemetery. He paused to watch, hidden in the shadows among the trees, enjoying the view as Russ moved with power and confidence. *His wolf is never far from the surface. I wonder if he sees the fox in me?*

At first, Liam thought Russ might just be out for a walk, looking for a bit of peace at the end of a busy day. But then he could see that Russ had a purpose, heading for one stone in particular.

Hmm. Who is he visiting? His mother? A friend? His fox nature craved knowledge, and it took all of Liam's restraint to keep from trotting over and sticking his pointy nose into Russ's business.

Russ hunkered down in front of a glossy black stone. His lips moved, but at this distance, even Liam's fox hearing couldn't pick up the words. Russ's one-sided conversation went on for a while. From the hunch of his shoulders and the way he kept his head bowed, every line of his body showed his grief.

Liam twitched his ears, a nervous habit. Russ's scent seemed different, heavier. Sad. An overwhelming need to comfort and protect swept over Liam, something he'd never felt before. His fox might be smaller and lighter than Russ's wolf, but he was just as much a predator, and he could be a fury of fangs and claws when necessary. Now, everything in him fought to be at his mate's side, steadying him and watching his back.

Mate, his fox snarled. *Our mate is in pain.*

If it were up to their animals, Liam wouldn't have doubted his presence was welcome. But their human sides also had a say, and no matter what Liam sensed about their connection and attraction, they were nearly strangers. He didn't have the right to intrude.

Finally, Russ stood. Perhaps his wolf caught Liam's scent, because he turned just as Liam tried to fade into the forest. Had he caught a glimpse? Liam waited until he was certain that Russ was gone.

He padded out into the fading light and made for the headstone where Russ had paid his respects.

Anthony Moretti, the stone read, with two intertwined hearts and the dates. Beneath that, *Beloved husband, gone too soon. Always remembered.*

Husband.

The thought sent a shock of emotion through him, strong enough to make him quiver. He'd expected the headstone to belong to a family member or a close friend, but not a partner. By the dates, Russ's late husband had been gone for two years, which was barely time to grieve so deep a loss.

He figured Russ to be in his early or mid-thirties, old enough that it shouldn't have come as a surprise that he had past relationships, serious ones. But...Russ had buried his husband. That was something Liam hadn't expected.

Maybe I'm not the only one with a difficult past or reasons why we should take this...whatever it is...slowly.

Husband isn't the same as mate, his fox reminded him.

No, but it's serious and real. It's one more reason to move carefully. If we're true mates, time is on our side.

Liam couldn't shake off his glum mood after the cemetery, despite how well the run had started. He slunk back to where he had left his clothes and dressed, minding the wind and cold more than when he had set out.

The grocery store was on his way, so Liam picked up a frozen pepperoni pizza for dinner, as well as some peanut butter, jelly, and bread for comfort. He promised himself a more thorough shopping trip when he had wrangled his feelings to a better place.

He let himself into the bungalow, stripped off his coat and boots, and pre-heated the oven. All the while, his mind spun. Picturing Russ with another partner made his fox want to scream and bark with jealousy. Getting his fox to settle down wasn't going to be easy. Arguing with his shifter side over primal topics required patience, and often took an appeal to emotion over mere words.

Liam couldn't think with his fox carrying on. He closed his eyes and breathed deeply, then sent images from memories to soothe his other half. He recalled how amazingly good it felt to be alone in the tow truck cab with Russ. How safe and protected he felt when Russ walked him home. The electricity that passed between them when their fingers brushed. And Liam's own sudden change of heart to cautiously admit there might be something to the whole "fated mates" idea.

Gradually, his fox calmed, no longer pacing or throwing himself in a fury against Liam's mental walls, although his tail lashed back and forth, signaling danger.

Russ invited me for coffee. So he at least wants to be friends...and I think he's interested in more. We both need to move slowly. Even if we truly are fated mates, our human sides need to be onboard as much as our shifter selves. So we'll start easy. Get to know each other. Go from there.

His fox glared balefully but didn't respond, something Liam took as a win. *Now, let me eat before I have a splitting headache.*

Liam spent a few hours after dinner researching fated mates. Unfortunately, most of what he found on the internet came from TV shows, movies, and books, so he doubted the accuracy. Liam did find some old resources in special collections his librarian credentials accessed; ones that appeared to be genuine. The scant information made it clear that fated mates were real, although relatively rare.

Liam's curiosity got the better of him, and he searched on Russ's name. He found the website for the auto shop, the deed for a cabin, and a social media page that hadn't been updated lately. The page didn't offer a lot of personal information, although several pictures of Russ and Drew horsing around made Liam smile. He did note the birthdate. *Libra, huh?*

While Liam had never placed a lot of stock in astrology or things like the tarot, he remembered from his classes with Jeffries that his mentor believed those forms of divination could be accurate when done by a skilled practitioner. On a whim, Liam looked up compatible signs.

I'm a Leo. He's a Libra. That's supposed to be the ideal combination. Maybe I should learn more about this. He bought an ebook on zodiac signs, figuring it couldn't hurt.

Liam made an early night of it after reading long enough to relax.

In the middle of the night, sirens woke him from a dead sleep, and he sat bolt upright, adrenaline pumping, heart thudding.

Shit. That's right. I now live next door to the fire department.

Another thought hit moments later, as sleep cleared from his mind.

Fuck. Russ is a firefighter. Please, let him be safe.

Liam went to his front window but saw no trace of smoke or fire.

He settled back under the covers once the sirens ended, but he couldn't get back to sleep, not with so much on his mind.

His cell phone rang at eight in the morning, and Liam eyed it like it was a snake. Only two people in Fox Hollow had his phone number, and there were very few folks from Ithaca he needed or wanted to talk to.

"Hello, Liam?" The voice sounded familiar, but definitely not either Russ or Jeffries.

"Who is this?" Liam tried not to sound defensive and realized he probably failed.

"Uh, this is Drew Lowe, Russ's brother. I got your number from the auto shop. Russ was called in this morning to spell the night shift at the firehouse, so he wanted me to tell you that he can't meet you for coffee this morning, but he'll call to set up a new time as soon as he's off-duty."

"Is he okay? I heard the sirens but couldn't see anything."

"Yeah," Drew replied. "He's part of the clean-up crew to make sure the blaze is out and that there's nothing dangerous leaking. I shouldn't say anything else since the details aren't public. But he made me swear to call you at eight sharp or risk an ass-whupping, so this is me, delivering the message."

"Thank you." Liam focused on the fact that Russ was all right. Relief flooded through him, strong enough to blunt the disappointment of the delayed date. "I really appreciate you calling—and that he thought of it, with all that going on."

Drew gave a short, sharp laugh. "That's my brother—he takes his commitments very seriously. So when he says he'll call—he *will* call."

4

RUSS

"You're sure it was arson?" Russ asked.

Fire Chief Saunders nodded, soot-streaked and exhausted. "Afraid so. I've notified the State Fire Marshal, who might send out an investigator. And I've got the police looking into it. I trust Sheriff Armel will get to the bottom of it. He's got friends in Albany who can expedite the testing if needed."

"Why would someone pick this place to burn?" Russ looked at the smoldering remains of what had been a modest summer cabin. Plenty of people came up to spend all or part of the season where cooler temperatures and a slower pace offered a chance to recharge. Around Fox Hollow, most of those people were shifters who valued being able to be themselves—their whole selves—somewhere safe.

"Don't know yet. But, like I said, it's got all the signs of having been set. What they did was effective—it's a textbook case, so whoever it was either didn't know how to be sneaky or didn't bother."

The chief moved on while Russ caught up with Ty, Justin, and the others who were hosing down the wreckage and checking to make sure there were no lurking hotspots or surprises buried in the rubble. He took his place on the line, falling into a familiar routine where he and his friends worked in well-practiced synchronicity.

The questions cycled in his mind. *Why would anyone want to burn this place? Can't have been worth much for insurance—and if they didn't even bother to be sneaky about it, they won't see any money.*

Revenge? It's a bit out of the way to make a point if someone had a score to settle. A family squabble? Someone didn't get what they wanted from an inheritance? Russ worked through all the reasons he could come up with, and none of them seemed to fit.

When was the last time we had arson— or any kind of blaze beyond someone lighting a garbage fire that got out of control?

In the ten years he had lived in Fox Hollow, Russ couldn't think of a single case. He knew all of the town's police officers and heard most of the scuttlebutt since they shared a building with the fire department. Every town had crime, but most of what happened in Fox Hollow paled by comparison to the bigger cities. Partly because the year-round residents all knew each other, and also because it was difficult to get away with too much surrounded by shifters and psychics, so the town wasn't a tempting target.

Why here, and why now?

Russ's wolf didn't like the possibility of an unknown danger, and his Libra nature demanded answers. He took any threat to his town and his "pack" of friends seriously.

And to our mate, his wolf reminded him.

Russ knew it was pointless to argue with his other half, especially when the wolf was right. As raw and real as his grief had been yesterday at Anthony's grave, the sheer fury that rose inside him at the thought of any harm to Liam just confirmed that they were truly fated mates.

Then I'd better help the chief get to the bottom of this.

By noon, his crew had finished all they could do at the scene. But they had barely returned to the firehouse and showered before a call came in for EMTs to deal with a near-drowning at Forked Lake, a popular campground. At least that was a win since the boy would likely be fine despite his close call.

"Go home," the chief said when the crew returned from the lake. "The next shift came in early. Get some rest. Nice work."

Russ walked out of the firehouse with Justin, Brandon, and Ty.

They looked as weary as he felt, and Russ knew that even after showering, they would all smell of smoke for a long while.

"Hey, Russ, want to come over to my place and watch a movie?" Brandon asked, making Russ realize he'd been lost in his thoughts.

"Sounds fun, but not today," he replied, torn between calling Liam to ask him to dinner and just walking half a block to knock on his door.

"Well, if you change your mind, you know where to find us," Brandon said, heading out with the others as Russ debated his next move.

He ended up calling and found himself pacing as he waited for Liam to pick up. "Liam? It's Russ. I'm so sorry I had to miss coffee this morning, but if you're free, I'd like to take you to dinner tonight."

"Are you okay? And yes, dinner sounds good."

Russ picked up a note of worry in Liam's voice that warmed his heart. "I'm fine, although I'm going to smell like smoke for a few days. Which means going somewhere casual tonight, but I'll absolutely give you a raincheck for somewhere fancier another time."

"I haven't been anywhere here except the coffee shop, so I'm open to new experiences," Liam assured him. "When do you want to go?"

"I can be on your front porch in five minutes. Too soon?"

Liam chuckled. "Works for me. I was just realizing it had been a long time since lunch."

Russ might have shaved a minute or two off that ETA, struggling to walk the line between "enthusiastic" and "stalker."

If you just brought him a nice, plump rabbit, it would be simpler, his wolf pointed out.

I'm too tired to hunt. Is there predator take-out?

His wolf sniffed, giving him a slit-eyed look of annoyance and padded off. Russ knocked on Liam's door, trying not to rock back and forth like a teenager on his first date.

"You weren't kidding on the time," Liam said with a grin, stepping out onto the porch and locking the door behind him. He wore a snug pair of jeans, hiking boots, and a dark green sweater over a button-down shirt that peeked through where his heavy coat hung open.

"I just finished my shift and got cleaned up next door," Russ replied with a jerk of his head to indicate the station, "Didn't think it made sense to go home and come in again." He ran a hand through his hair self-consciously. "Sorry if I smell like a day-old campfire."

Liam sniffed the air playfully, then leaned closer for a deeper inhale to catch Russ's scent. Russ's heart sped when Liam wanted to scent him, a clear indication of interest. He caught a whiff of Liam as well and felt that connection go right to his cock.

"You smell just fine to me," Liam said, with a twinkle of mischief in his amber eyes and a flirty wink.

"Diner okay?" Russ asked, to keep himself from overstepping since what he really wanted to do was crowd Liam up against the door and kiss him long and slow.

I will not act like a caveman just because of some stupid hormones. Fated mate or not, we are going to do this in a civilized fashion, he told himself sternly. He felt certain that wolves couldn't actually snicker, but his certainly seemed to be trying.

The diner was just up the street and around the corner, across from The Lone Coyote gift and book shop.

"Have you been to the Coyote yet?" Russ asked, gesturing to the big store on the corner. "It's kind of a Fox Hollow landmark."

Liam eyed the building's somewhat garish sign, emblazoned with a howling coyote, then took in the multitude of dreamcatchers hanging in the windows. "I figured it was a tourist trap."

Russ laughed. "Oh, it is—but in the best way. The Thompson family's owned it for a couple of generations, and every few years they find a way to build on yet another extension. The touristy stuff is up front. They also have a nice selection of T-shirts, an impressive book section with local authors and area history, and a decent stock of DVDs, since not everyone around here streams everything. Jewelry too—and not the cheap stuff."

"Huh. Guess I'll have to take a look around," Liam replied.

"Plus the Thompsons are big supporters of the summer arts programs and the Fall Fling," Russ tossed out, knowing that would catch Liam's interest. "They're good people."

"Now I know I need to do my Christmas shopping there," Liam said, but his smile quickly faded. Russ wondered if that meant Liam didn't have anyone to shop for.

I plan to fix that, he thought.

"Becker's Bar and Grill has good food, too," Russ added as they crossed Route 28 toward the Full Moon Diner. "But it's always a little warm and crowded in there, and I think everyone will breathe a little easier with my smoke-stink if we go somewhere else tonight. The diner isn't fancy, but the menu is all comfort food."

"Full Moon, huh?"

Russ shrugged. "We hide in plain sight around here."

When they reached the diner, Russ opened the door for Liam, and his hand fell to the small of Liam's back as they entered. He hadn't meant to do either of those things, but the actions came naturally, and to Russ's relief, Liam didn't pull away.

"Hiya, Russ. Who's your friend?" A jovial-looking man with a round face and stocky body greeted Russ from behind the counter.

"Liam Reynard, meet Woody Adamson—he owns this fine dining establishment. Woody, this is Liam, our new head librarian."

Woody lifted his head to peer at Liam, probably trying to get a better look through his bifocals. "Librarian, huh? Welcome. Russ can give you the run-down on everything we serve. He and Drew are two of our best customers." His gaze darted from Liam to Russ, but he didn't ask, and Russ felt relieved at not having to figure out what to say.

"Go find a seat, and we'll bring out menus," Woody told them. "Maxine's meatloaf is the special of the day, and the apple pie just came out of the oven."

Russ led Liam to a booth near the back where the din of conversation and the clink of dishes wouldn't make it hard to talk. The red vinyl booths had a retro flair, just like the rest of the diner.

"I like it already," Liam said as he slid in across from Russ.

"You can't go wrong, no matter what you pick. The meatloaf is pretty awesome, and the onion rings are hand-cut and dipped. The pie is amazing. If most of the town didn't have shifter metabolisms, we'd all be totally chonky," Russ admitted.

"So, Woody is…"

"Woodchuck shifter," Russ said.

"And the people who own the big gift shop?"

"I'll give you one guess, and "coyote" doesn't count."

"Wow. You weren't kidding about hiding in plain sight," Liam replied.

Russ couldn't decipher the expression that crossed Liam's face.

"I've never had that luxury," Liam continued. "It'll take a little getting used to."

"I don't imagine folks were open about it, down in Ithaca," Russ said.

Liam shook his head. "No. And no one would have believed it, even if we'd tried to tell them. I knew a couple of other shifters, but that was only because we happened upon each other out in the woods."

Russ felt a stab of sadness for all that Liam must have missed out on, not having other shifters around. "That's one of the best things about Fox Hollow, in my opinion. Folks here look out for each other, and we take care of our own."

For a second, he saw a glimpse of something lost and longing in Liam's eyes, and his wolf wanted nothing more than to wrap around him and let him know that he had a home and a pack.

Jumping the gun, he warned both sides of himself. *Take it slow.*

"You and Drew came here from somewhere else, right? Were there shifters where you lived before?"

Conversation paused as their server brought menus and glasses of water. Russ was happy for the reprieve, which gave him a moment to think about how he wanted to frame the circumstances that brought him to town.

Tell him the truth. You've got nothing to be ashamed of. Your birth pack was dishonorable, his wolf prodded.

Maybe so, but being thrown out isn't something to brag about.

Hmpf, the wolf sniffed. *You should have just peed on them before walking away.*

"My pack didn't take it well when I came out," Russ said. "They told me to leave. Drew refused to stay without me. It's been the two of us against the world since then."

"How did you end up here?"

Russ gave a rueful smile. "A family friend heard about what

happened and offered us his place. We bought it and fixed it up, and bought into the auto shop when it went up for sale."

"Sounds like it was meant to be," Liam said, with a smile Russ thought was adorable.

Russ thought about how beautiful the red fox had been that he'd glimpsed in the cemetery. He felt certain that had been Liam. If so, his fox was every bit as gorgeous as the man himself.

"Do I have something stuck in my teeth?" Liam asked, and Russ realized he'd been staring.

"No. Sorry. I just got lost in my head for a minute." Russ hoped Liam didn't interpret his zoning out as lack of interest. "It's been a busy day."

"Thank you for getting together for dinner, after all that. I would have understood if you needed to postpone."

Russ met Liam's gaze. "I was looking forward to spending time with you. And I figured we both needed to eat. Plus, I wanted to introduce you to the wonderful cuisine in your new home town." His last comment lightened the mood, but Russ swore he saw a flash of interest in Liam's eyes.

Liam went for the fried chicken on Russ's recommendation, while Russ ordered the meatloaf. Both men reserved slices of apple pie for dessert.

"How did your day go?" Russ asked, hoping Liam was settling in.

"Pretty well," Liam replied. "I got my things put away, and took a little stroll around town. Then I picked up coffee at Bear Necessities, and walked down and drank it on the beach."

"Nice. That's a great way to start the day."

"Stopped for groceries on the way home, so I won't starve for a few days," Liam added. "I can't live without my PB&J. Most perfect combination in the universe." He sighed. "And then I did some internet searching on the summer and fall festivals in Fox Hollow over the last couple of years. They look fantastic. Walter must have been a pretty amazing organizer."

Russ nodded. "He was, and Linda and Maddi also get a lot of the credit. Both programs have a huge turnout—from locals and tourists. That helps the businesses in town, but it also helps to spotlight the summer arts program from the schools and community college, and the programs from Fox Institute. It's a win all the way around."

Liam tapped his fingers on the table. "It's exciting to continue something so successful and try to come up with ways to keep it fresh without changing its core."

"Do you have ideas?" Russ couldn't help being curious. As good as the two events were, the last couple of years had been largely repeats given Walter's declining health.

"Some, but I don't want to be the new guy who thinks he's got all the answers," Liam replied. "So I want to sit down with Linda and Maddi—and Dr. Jeffries—and see what other people have been thinking. We're doing that tomorrow morning, and I'm pretty excited about it."

Russ could see the enthusiasm in Liam's expression and thought it boded well. *If he likes his job, he'll stay. And we can figure things out.*

If you just claim him as your fated mate and bite him, he'll stay, and there's a lot less to figure out, his wolf noted.

"Alright, boys. I hope you're hungry," their server said. She was a motherly woman with short dark hair, probably one of Woody's many relations, Russ thought.

Liam took a bite of fried chicken, and Russ couldn't take his gaze off those pink lips and sharp teeth. *Fox and the henhouse,* his wolf snarked.

"Oh, my God, you were right about the chicken," Liam said after he had swallowed. "That is some of the best I've ever had."

"You should try a bite of my meatloaf," Russ replied. "Give me your spoon." He used the clean utensil to scoop up a corner of his piece, making sure to get some of the tangy sauce as well as the fresh-made mashed potatoes. Russ held out the spoon for Liam, expecting the other man to take it from him, but instead, Liam leaned across the table and ate the bite, then sat back and licked his lips.

"I might never cook again," Liam said, with a pornographic little moan of delight that made Russ shift in his seat.

"I know, right? There's a reason this place has been around for a while—and it's all family recipes."

Conversation lagged as both men dug into their food, but they were hungry, so it didn't take long to clean their plates. Cheryl, their server, had dessert in front of them practically before they had set down their forks.

"The pie is still warm enough to melt the ice cream. Woody threw the à la mode in for free, to welcome our new librarian," she added with a grin directed at Liam.

"Thank you—and please tell Woody 'thanks' as well," Liam replied.

If watching Liam eat chicken sent all kinds of naughty thoughts to Russ's cock, apple pie with ice cream made those ideas even more explicit. Liam licked the creamy white dribbles of melted ice cream off his lips with a flick of his pink tongue, and the expressions he made at the taste of the pie, as well as the way he let his head fall back to expose his throat as he swallowed, had Russ painfully hard in his jeans.

He had been so busy taking in the show—and he had the feeling Liam knew exactly what he was doing—that his own pie remained unfinished.

"Go ahead. It's too good to waste," Liam said with a smile, watching Russ with equally rapt interest that made him feel both desired and self-conscious.

When Cheryl brought the bill, they both reached for it, and once again, Russ felt a tingle race from where their fingers met all the way up his arm. From the look on Liam's face, he felt the same thing.

"Let me," Russ said, not moving his hand away. "Since I was the one who asked, and I stood you up this morning."

Liam tilted his head, sending a lock of red hair into his eyes, which made him look like his fox. "If you insist. But I get the next one."

Russ's heart sped at the idea of there being a "next one." "Sounds good to me."

He settled the check, and they headed back into town. When they reached the bungalow's porch, Liam gave a shy smile. "Would you like to come in for a beer? I picked some up when I got groceries."

Russ might have been completely exhausted, but he wasn't going to turn down Liam's offer. "I'd love to."

They left their boots and coats in the front entranceway, and Russ followed Liam into the kitchen. The Arts and Crafts style of the outside carried through to the details on the inside, helping to make the small house both charming and cozy.

"Apologies if Black Bear Brewing isn't your first choice, but I thought I should work my way through the local brews, and it was the pack I saw first." Liam pulled out a bottle, popped off the cap, and handed it to Russ, unmistakably brushing their fingers together. He readied a bottle for himself and led Russ into the living room.

"Are you kidding? It's one of my favorites." Russ followed Liam to sit on the couch, close but not too close, taking his cues from his host, although Russ would have preferred to be pressed together from knee to hip.

"Really? Oh, good." Liam said with a bright smile. He took a long drink, once again giving Russ a great view of his neck and the way his throat moved as he swallowed, which conjured up plenty of ideas. He licked the foam from his lips, meeting Russ's gaze. "That is pretty awesome."

"I'm glad you like it," Russ said. "And I'm very glad you're here in Fox Hollow." He cleared his throat. "Look, I know you haven't been here in town long, and you're just settling in, but...I'd like to see you again."

Liam hesitated, and Russ's heart sank. Then Liam seemed to settle his internal debate, and nodded, with a touch of that shy smile Russ found so endearing. "I'd like that."

They chatted as they drank their beer, and Russ thought about how comfortable it felt to be here, like this, as if he and Liam had known each other forever. He had always disliked dating, hating the awkwardness and the disappointment, but with Liam, things just felt right.

"You're easy to talk to," Liam said, finishing off the last of his beer. "That's...nice."

Russ's bottle was already empty, and he leaned forward to put it on the coffee table just as Liam did the same. That brought them close enough to bump shoulders, with their faces only inches apart. They stilled; gazes locked.

"I really want to kiss you," Russ breathed. "May I?"

Liam nodded, never breaking eye contact. "Yes," he murmured, barely above a whisper.

Russ leaned in and brushed his lips against Liam's, gentle and careful. Liam moved to deepen the kiss, and Russ brought his hand up to stroke Liam's cheek. Liam pressed into Russ's palm, kissing back with intent.

Liam's tongue flicked against Russ's lips, and Russ let him in, intrigued that Liam took the lead. Most of the men Russ had dated just assumed that because he was tall and muscular—and a wolf shifter—he would automatically want to be in charge. He did—sometimes. That had been something he'd appreciated about his relationship with Anthony, that it had been equal in every way.

He'd expected that thoughts of his late husband would dim his mood, but to his surprise they didn't. Instead, a sense of calm certainty flooded over him, reinforcing his gut feeling that this was the right thing to do.

Liam's tongue explored Russ's mouth, taking his time. Russ changed the angle of the kiss and let his tongue slide over Liam's soft lips, lapping and licking, finding his sensitive places.

Russ slipped an arm around Liam's shoulders, pulling him closer, and Liam obliged, pressing up against his side. Liam's hands slid down Russ's chest, tracing the cut of his muscles. Russ cradled Liam's face with one broad palm, but let his other hand run down Liam's arm, finding strong muscles that added to the image his imagination supplied of Liam without a shirt.

Their kisses turned breathless and hungry. Russ brought his hand up to run his fingers through Liam's red hair. Liam's hands moved across Russ's shoulders, down his arms, then over his chest again, as if he were mapping and memorizing every inch.

Liam crawled onto Russ's lap, one knee on each side of his thighs, never breaking their kiss. Russ slid his hands down Liam's back, then cupped his toned ass and brought him close enough to feel their erections press together in delicious friction.

If he had any doubts about Liam being on board, the way he ground against him answered the question. Russ kissed his way down Liam's face, from his cheekbones down the line of his jaw, then to his lips again, savoring a few more moments. By this time of the day, both of them sported enough stubble to add a sexy scrape when they moved against each other, which Russ had to admit had always been a turn on.

Liam moaned and arched back, changing the angle of their cocks and baring that beautiful length of throat. Russ accepted the invitation and explored the expanse of skin, licking and kissing, aware of the pulse beneath his lips and the heady rush of Liam's scent.

"What do you want?" Russ asked quietly, not sure how far either of them were ready to take this, prepared to step away if Liam had already reached his limit, but hoping for more.

Liam gave a throaty chuckle. "I want to come and make you come, but I'd rather not cream my pants." He rubbed them together again to make his point, and Russ fought back a growl.

Russ brought his hand between them, going to the buckle of Liam's belt. "This okay?" he murmured, as he moved to work it open.

"Yes. Please." The sheer want in Liam's voice made Russ catch his breath.

Russ opened Liam's fly, and Liam shifted to allow Russ to push his jeans and briefs down his thighs and then take hold of his hard, dripping cock. He couldn't see much from this angle, but he liked the feel, steel beneath velvet, uncut.

Liam fumbled with Russ's jeans, pushing them down until he could get his lover's cock in hand, and Russ caught his breath, overwhelmed by sensation. He hadn't felt the touch of any but his own hand since… and now he realized how much he had missed that connection.

Russ brought their cocks together in his larger hand, and Liam helped complete the grip, forming a pre-come slicked tunnel for them to fuck into, rubbing against Russ's calloused palm and Liam's softer skin.

Liam had one hand on Russ's shoulder, steadying himself as he rutted into the channel of their hands. Russ bucked his hips, matching him stroke for stroke, unable to take his eyes off how Liam's sinewy body moved in an erotic dance.

"Oh!" Liam's climax seemed to catch him by surprise, and his whole body went rigid, head thrown back, thighs clamping tightly against Russ's hips as he shot over their joined hands.

Russ was just a few strokes behind him, crying out with his release, adding his come to Liam's.

Liam fell forward, resting his forehead on Russ's shoulder. Russ knew he would keep that image of Liam in his mind forever—mussed hair, wide eyes, mouth open, and an expression of fucked-out bliss on his face—a look Russ had put there.

Russ still panted from the strength of his climax. Then he reached forward with his clean hand and tipped Liam's chin up to kiss him gently and thoroughly. The room smelled of sweat, sex, and their mingled scents, a completely intoxicating mixture.

Fated mates, his wolf reminded him. *If you think this is good, just wait—*

"Wow." Liam's voice sounded a little spacey. Russ could relate. He felt buzzed, far more than he could blame on a single beer.

"Yeah." Russ spotted a box of tissues on the end table and grabbed a couple, doing his best to clean them up.

Russ tossed the used tissues onto the floor and ran his fingers through Liam's hair again. "You're so gorgeous," he murmured. "And so is your fox. I saw you out at the cemetery."

Liam's amber eyes met his, and Russ thought he saw a flash of pride mingled with uncertainty. "I wondered if you had. I saw you too. And the marker."

Was there ever a good time to discuss your dead husband with your new lover? "Yeah. I probably should have mentioned that earlier."

Liam kissed him again before he could get further. "It's not like we've had a lot of time. This thing between us...moving so fast...it's not the way it usually goes for me."

Russ returned the kiss gently. "There hasn't been anyone since Anthony died. Car wreck. I got called to the scene before they knew who was involved."

"Damn. I'm sorry."

Russ looked away. "He was already gone. We were good together, and I loved him. But he wasn't my fated mate."

He dared to meet Liam's gaze on those last words and saw a flash of understanding. *He knows,* Russ's wolf assured him.

"I didn't used to think that was real," Liam murmured. "But I've never felt anything like this before."

"We can take it slow," Russ assured him, wishing he could read minds. If Liam backed out now, Russ didn't know what he would do. "There's no rush. Get to know each other. Date. That way, we can be sure."

Liam nodded and swallowed hard. "I'd like that." He tensed, and Russ wasn't sure what to expect. "I had a boyfriend back in Ithaca. We'd been together for a while. Then things went bad fast. I think he—"

The shrill alarm made both men startle, and Russ sighed as he pulled his phone from his pocket. "It's the fire station. Another fire. I'm sorry—but I have to go."

Liam kissed him and then wriggled off of his lap, and they both pulled themselves together. Russ went to the bathroom to wash up, knowing that even so, his shifter buddies would be able to smell the sex on him.

"Be safe," Liam said as Russ headed for the door.

Russ gave him a quick kiss and met his gaze. "I'll do my best. I'm gonna be wiped out after this, but I'll call, and we'll go out again real soon, I promise."

Liam nodded, biting his lip with a worried expression as he closed the door behind him.

As soon as he was off the porch, Russ called in. "What's going on?"

"Get here as quick as you can," the Chief replied. "We've got what looks like another arson."

5

LIAM

A MIND-BLOWING ORGASM SHOULD HAVE BEEN THE PRELUDE TO A SOUND night's sleep. Instead, Liam lay awake that night, replaying the evening with Russ, and reliving the "happy ending." He'd never come so hard just from frotting.

If that was amazing, what would it be like to do more? His imagination teemed with possibilities, removing any doubt that might still exist about whether his libido had recovered.

Fated mates, his fox replied, smugly.

That was great sex...but it was more than great sex. Liam had tried casual hookups in college and tired of it quickly. Someone with enthusiasm and a good grasp of the mechanics of sex could be a great fuck. As good as that felt, Liam had always hated the let-down later, going home alone, waiting for a call that never came.

But this hadn't felt anything like those quickies, even though he and Russ had only known each other a few days. *And it was better than any of the sex Kelson and I ever had,* he admitted to himself.

Liam had dated Kelson for more than a year, but it should have been a red flag that their relationship never moved beyond convenient sex. They had been boyfriends, but Kelson showed no interest in taking things further, moving in together, committing. Looking back,

Liam realized that for as bad as their breakup was, it would have been worse if they had stayed together.

Catching Kelson cheating had made Liam question everything he thought he knew, and doubt his own ability to read people, even with his shifter senses and the talent his Leo birth sign supposedly had in that regard. Kelson had been unfaithful, and Liam suspected that the guy he caught his boyfriend with wasn't the first. Still, Kelson had twisted everything to make it all Liam's fault, and when Liam had stood up to him, it got nasty.

Kelson had stalked him, posted pictures online Liam hadn't known about and trashed him on social media. Finally, Liam obtained a restraining order and then suddenly Kelson went silent.

Liam hoped it meant Kelson had lost interest. *Instead, he was hiring a hitman.*

He meant it when he had sworn off men. And then Russ showed up. Suddenly, everything Liam thought he knew about himself and his shifter side had changed.

I thought fated mates were just in romance books. But I can't deny what I feel when I'm with Russ, and the feeling seems mutual.

That's because he's not a dumbass, his fox snarked. *He's not fighting finding his mate. He'd probably love to bite you if you'd let him.*

Were mating bites even real? Liam wondered. *And if they were, did they create the kind of bond he'd read about in those steamy books?*

One way to find out, his fox said.

Liam stared at the ceiling, trying to sort out the storm of conflicting feelings threatening to burst out of his chest. *I'm not fighting it. I just need to understand. Be sure. I was so wrong about Kelson—*

Did anything with that mangy cur feel at all like just touching Russ does? His fox had never liked Kelson, but at the time, Liam had been ignoring his other half—which was a mistake. Even if he did once confess the truth about being a shifter to Kelson in a misguided moment of trust. Of course Kelson had mocked him, believing none of it.

But he must have believed. Or else he wouldn't have hired a Huntsman.

Liam realized he hadn't answered his fox. *No. This doesn't feel like it did with Kelson. Not at all. I just wish everything wasn't happening at once — the move, Russ, new job, and maybe a contract on my head.*

Another reason why having a protective wolf isn't a bad idea.

Liam sighed. *I wish I knew whether that hitman is still after me. I should tell the cops — and Russ. And Jeffries. But tell them what? I've got no details about who the guy was who came after me. I can't prove it. If Jeb found out more, he'd have let me know.*

His friend Jeb was also a shifter and had warned him about the Huntsman, since Liam had remained friends with a few people who stayed in touch with Kelson. Apparently, Kelson had been on a bender and bragged about putting out the hit to a friend, who made sure Jeb knew. Jeb had heard the legends about Huntsmen and took the threat seriously. With Jeb's warning, Liam had barely escaped.

I'm overthinking the best sex of my life. I need to sleep, start my new job, and take things one day at a time.

Even so, Liam lay awake for a long while, waiting to hear the fire trucks return. *Please let him be all right,* he begged the universe. He finally fell asleep, but the trucks still weren't back.

HIS FIRST OFFICIAL day at the library turned out to be a success. Linda and Maddi were sharp, creative, and excited about possibilities. Their brainstorming session had them all humming with energy and new ideas, and by the end of the day, they had worked up a plan for the summer and opportunities for the fall.

Liam came home jittery as fuck. He had a text from Russ letting him know he'd gotten in safely during the wee hours, but that he was wiped out and going to sleep. That left Liam on his own, and he decided that another run in his fur was what he needed.

This time, he thought he would run somewhere a little farther afield. Liam entered the woods behind the new section of the cemetery and went away from town, through a stretch of forest, past a motel and an old, refurbished mansion, and then into another patch of woods behind a small lakeside cluster of summer cabins.

He raised his face to the wind, letting the breeze ruffle his fur and his whiskers.

That's when he smelled smoke.

Fuck. There've been two arsons in the past couple of days. What are the odds this is another one?

Just remember darling, fur is flammable, his fox warned.

Without his phone, there wasn't any way to warn anyone. That meant Liam would have to do recon old school.

It'll be easy. Just get close and get out. Even if someone sees me, no one suspects a fox.

Except in a town filled with shifters, his fox reminded him.

Liam stayed low, keeping to the tree line as long as he could, following his nose to find the source of the smoke. The first three cabins looked locked tight for the off-season. The fourth had a motorcycle parked in back, and while the windows were still boarded shut for the winter, the back door stood open.

He crouched, knowing this was where the smoke originated, and that meant the biker was responsible. His nose twitched with the smell of smoke…and lighter fluid. Liam belly-crawled as close as he dared in the tall grass, focusing his fox-sharp senses to pick up any clue that might help catch the person.

Minutes later, a large man in a black leather bike jacket, jeans, and boots came out—wearing leather gloves and a full helmet. *I can't be sure, but he has the same overall build as the Huntsman who came after me in Ithaca.*

Liam had no chance to see the man's face or get any description except his build, although he memorized the stranger's scent. He had already memorized the make, model, and license plate of the bike.

The man paused and looked around, likely reassuring himself that no one was watching. Liam flattened himself to the ground, ready to bolt if discovered. He lay still, heart thudding, until the bike roared away.

The cabin exploded into flames. Liam didn't know much about fighting fires, but he knew this was far more than he could handle with a fire extinguisher.

As soon as Liam knew the motorcycle was gone, he ran as fast as his fox feet could carry him, back through the woods the way he came, pelting through the underbrush. He almost ran straight for the fire department and remembered at the last minute that he needed to be human to report the fire, so he stopped long enough to shift and dress. Then he sprinted across the street to report the fire.

"Can I help you?" A man in a FHFD T-shirt answered his frantic knock.

"There's a cabin on fire, over that way," Liam said, still breathless. Belatedly, he realized that he didn't know the names of the streets in his new town, and so all he could do was gesture. "Is Russ here?"

The man shook his head. "He put in a long day. Can you tell me what you saw?"

Liam forced himself to breathe. "I went out for a run," he told the firefighter. "I'm new in town—just been here a few days—so I don't know the names of anything. But I smelled smoke, so I went to see where it came from, and there was a man on a motorcycle coming out of the house that's on fire."

"Shit," the firefighter said. He ran a hand back through his short-trimmed dark hair. "Stay here. I gotta call the chief, and I'll put in an alarm."

The piercing wail of the fire siren made Liam's fox yip in pain. *In a town full of shifters, how is everyone not deaf from that racket?*

He sat, nervously drumming his fingers. Sooner than he expected, a man in a fire chief uniform strode up and stopped in front of him. "Buck said you reported a fire—and maybe got a look at our arsonist?"

Liam fleetingly wondered if "Buck" referred to the firefighter's shifter side. He repeated his story nearly word for word, and the chief listened intently.

"I should tell you that was reckless and dangerous, and you shouldn't have done it," the chief said, then rolled his eyes and sighed. "But it's the first solid lead we've had. So thank you. Although next time—"

"Call a professional," Liam supplied, wondering if anyone would ever make a fox-friendly cell phone.

He left the firehouse, feeling hungry and a little disoriented. What he wanted was Russ, who was sleeping off back-to-back shifts. Instead, he found himself heading back to the Full Moon Diner, where Woody greeted him with a smile.

"Back already? Did you decide to get the meatloaf this time?"

Liam's amazement at being remembered as a customer, let alone having his order noted, must have shown in his face.

"We do our best to know what people like," Woody said. "Makes them feel at home."

"It's working," Liam replied with a tired smile. "And after the taste I had of the meatloaf last night, I'd love my own serving."

Cheryl guided him to a booth for two, in the thick of the dinner crowd. "You expecting anyone?" she asked, clearly meaning Russ.

"Not tonight," Liam replied ruefully.

"Well, then that means you don't have to share your dessert," Cheryl said with a broad wink. "'Sides, you've got one of the best seats in the house to hear everything that goes on, as much as anything ever does here. You'll know all the local news by the time you're done eating and maybe some of the gossip too."

Liam settled in, ready to put Cheryl's prediction to the test. He tuned in to the voices around him, picking up snatches of conversation.

"… say it's going to be an early winter. Someday it'll just stay winter all the time."

"… I'll take snow over deer flies any day."

"… when the rain stops. Can't fly planes when it's raining."

"… two more missing hikers, can you believe that?"

Liam's focus honed in on those voices at the table behind him.

"What I'd like to know is, how does a lynx get lost in the woods?"

"Or an ocelot. This is what happens when you're too domesticated."

"They probably just went feral for a while," the first speaker said. "They'll wander back out when they get tired of playing wild kitty."

The conversation shifted, and nothing else Liam overheard caught his attention, although he did learn about family squabbles, motorboat engines, and more than he ever wanted to know about fishing competitions.

Many of the other patrons drifted off as Liam ate his dinner, deep in thought. *Both the arsons and the missing hikers are unusual, according to what everyone's saying. Could they be related?*

Liam had always loved reading mysteries, and he had a weakness for watching detective series. Solving a mystery was like figuring out a puzzle, and in both his human and his fox form, Liam had always been good at puzzles.

Even worse, could both situations be connected to me? I show up and people start going missing and shit starts catching on fire. Seems like a big coincidence.

Before he could talk himself out of it, Liam grabbed his phone and dialed Jeffries at his office. He didn't feel right trying the man's home number, but it wasn't that late—his former professor could easily still be finishing up at the Institute.

Jeffries answered on the second ring. "Liam? Is something wrong?"

Psychic, Liam reminded himself, surprised that Jeffries would immediately begin with the assumption there was a problem. "I know it's late, but I have something important I need to talk to someone about and…well…"

"Come on by. The main front door to the building is still open until eight. Do you remember where to find my office?"

"Yes. I'll be there in about ten minutes. Thank you."

Liam ordered a piece of apple pie to go as a "thank you" present and headed over toward the Institute. A few cars passed on Route 28, but Saranac Road through "downtown" Fox Hollow was quiet. He turned to walk down the drive that led back to the schools, professional offices, and the Institute. Most of those buildings were dark now, and the parking lots were empty. Liam felt a shiver as he realized how isolated the area was after business hours.

This was a bad idea. Maybe I should have driven. If someone jumped me, there's no one to see.

Liam picked up his pace, keeping a wary eye out for trouble. A prickle at the back of his neck told him he was being watched, but he saw no one—either human or animal—and nothing stirred in the darkened windows of the buildings.

At least the parking lots were well lit, and Liam wondered if the buildings had security cameras. He castigated himself for being so foolish and taking chances. Then again, he had walked everywhere on Ithaca's campus by himself and never felt unsafe day or night.

But that wasn't true for everyone, he reminded himself. He had seen plenty of posters warning students to avoid lonely areas or dark short cuts. And he'd heard stories about campus crime. He just hadn't thought it would ever happen to him.

Just like I never thought anyone would send a Huntsman after me.

Liam couldn't stop a sigh of relief when he reached the bright lights of the main Institute building's entrance and found the door unlocked. He sniffed the air, alert for danger, and made sure he checked all around before heading up the stairs toward Jeffries's office.

He felt better noticing that several small groups of people were clustered in the Institute's main lobby seating area, talking or working on what looked like group projects. When he reached the second-floor offices, Liam heard voices carrying from behind doors left ajar and guessed the faculty were either catching up on phone calls or chatting with each other.

Jeffries's door was open wide and welcoming. He caught the fragrant smell of jasmine tea and wondered if Jeffries anticipated Liam's ragged nerves.

"Liam. Come in. I just made tea. Would you like some? It's herbal, so it shouldn't keep you up at night," Jeffries said with a smile.

"That sounds wonderful, thank you," Liam replied, taking a seat in one of the two chairs that faced the big wooden desk. Jeffries brought him a mug, then returned to pour one for himself and settled into the chair next to Liam, who handed over the piece of apple pie.

"I brought this from the diner," Liam said. "Thanks for meeting with me so late."

Jeffries grinned. "Diner pie is fantastic. Thank you so much." He set the box to the side and leaned forward after they both had time to take a few sips. "Now, what's got you worried?"

Liam took a deep breath, hoping that his confession wouldn't get him fired. "I'm afraid that the arsons and the missing hikers are related —and maybe connected to me."

Instead of immediately protesting, Jeffries's eyes narrowed in consideration. "What makes you think that?"

"There's a reason I was in such a hurry to leave Ithaca," Liam admitted. "In fact, I was already in my car on my way when I called to accept the job offer. I ran for my life with what I could carry because my ex-boyfriend hired a Huntsman to kill me."

Jeffries frowned. "I foresaw serious danger. Unfortunately, my abilities don't fill in a lot of details. How do you know he hired a Huntsman? And what does that have to do with arson and missing people?"

Liam told his story, not leaving out any details. "I barely made it out the window before he was breaking in my door," Liam concluded, feeling a whole-body tremor that had nothing to do with the temperature in the office.

"Hear me out," he said, raising a hand when Jeffries moved to object, probably to tell him that Huntsmen were just boogeyman legends. He felt even more resolve knowing that his friend had used the term "Huntsman," when he'd warned him.

"The two hikers who just went missing—one was an ocelot, and the other was a lynx. Those would be rare shifters...valuable to the wrong sort of people."

"Suppose you're right," Jeffries said slowly. "What do the fires have to do with anything?"

Liam shrugged. "Distractions. Tie up the first responders—the police and the firefighters—so they can't spend as much time looking for missing people."

"The Huntsmen—if they exist—aren't hitmen. They're more like traffickers who acquire supernatural creatures or people with special abilities for rich clients," Jeffries said, and Liam realized his mentor was taking him seriously.

"Right. Foxes have always been popular hunting targets," Liam replied, his lip curling in disdain. "The other two would be quite a prize."

"It would take a lot of balls to kidnap shifters in a place like Fox Hollow," Jeffries mused. "They're not the minority, and they aren't loners who have to hide. Not to mention that you've got a campus full of psychics."

"I thought about that," Liam replied. "You knew I was going to be in danger, but you didn't know details about how or from what. Have any of the psychics here picked up warning signals that they haven't been able to link to something? Or maybe a Huntsman knows how to block being seen by a witch or a psychic."

"That's not easy to do," Jeffries said, brows furrowed like he was trying to make the pieces fit together. "It's also not common knowledge."

"But if Huntsmen exist, wouldn't it stand to reason that they would have access to occult resources since they're hunting supernatural beings? Maybe they have some abilities of their own. It wouldn't be the first time someone turned against their group to make a buck," Liam replied.

"You make a good argument," Jeffries said. "But even if you're right, we don't have proof. From what I've heard about Sheriff Armel, he's fair, but he wants evidence. If we go in there talking about Huntsmen and hired assassins with nothing to base it on, he'll very politely toss us out on our asses."

Liam sagged in his chair. "That's what I was afraid you might say."

Jeffries leaned back, drumming the fingers of his right hand on his thigh. "I know that some of our faculty have been called in to help find people who go missing in the woods. It's pretty much standard protocol, at least around Fox Hollow. Let me do a little nosing around and see what they know. If it turns out that these last couple of disappearances aren't trackable in some strange way, I'd bet that's worth mentioning to the police."

"Thank you," Liam said quietly, suddenly feeling exhausted. "And thanks for not just laughing in my face."

"You were always one of my best students," Jeffries replied with a smile. "Your essays were well-reasoned, and you made a good case for your conclusions. Believe me, I'm taking this very seriously."

"I'm scared," Liam admitted. "I don't want to get killed. But I also don't want to be what attracts a Huntsman to Fox Hollow. Other people could get hurt because of me."

Jeffries tilted his head, looking intently at Liam. "You're wondering whether or not you should run away."

Liam nodded glumly. "I don't want to leave. I like the library and

Fox Hollow." *And Russ.* "But I don't want to bring trouble down on your heads."

Jeffries reached out to lay a hand on Liam's shoulder. "Please stay. You're safer here among us than on your own. We'll figure this out—together." He smiled. "And I believe a certain wolf shifter would be terribly disappointed."

Liam looked up sharply, then blushed. "That's another reason I don't want to leave."

"Promise me you'll give us a chance to deal with this?"

"I promise." He debated with himself for a moment before he added, "Would you mind driving me home, please? I got creeped out walking across the parking lots."

Jeffries got that assessing look again as if he understood what Liam really meant. "Of course. I was just wrapping things up for the night when you called. There's never an end to the tasks if you know what I mean."

"Thank you," Liam replied. "For everything."

"That's what friends are for," Jeffries assured him.

The drive back to Liam's house took only minutes by car, but he felt relieved not to need to cross the empty parking lots on foot. Jeffries parked in his driveway and turned to him. "I'm going to wait until you're safely inside. Someone meant you harm in Ithaca, and if there's any chance that you're right on this Huntsman thing, you need to not take any chances."

"I promise I'll be careful."

"You might consider telling Russ what you told me. He's a good guy, and you can count on him to have your back."

"Thank you," Liam said, planning to figure out when to tell Russ after he'd had a chance to sort out his thoughts. "I'll talk to you soon."

Liam restrained himself from running from the car to his door. He had his key already in hand and felt grateful that his porch light was on a timer, so he had a good view of the area. Liam opened and slipped inside, quickly locking it behind him and then waving from the window to assure Jeffries all was well.

Tomorrow, we need to go talk to the foxes. Maybe they've seen something. And if they haven't yet, maybe they will, Liam told his fox-self.

The dubious sniff he got in return let him know what his fox thought of getting to know the "locals." Admittedly, the "real" foxes back in Ithaca had been wary, but otherwise not bad sorts. He hoped that perhaps those here in the wild state forest might be easier to approach.

Liam checked his phone, hoping for a text from Russ, without luck. Then again, he hoped Russ had slept the whole day, recovering from the fires.

If there is a Huntsman, and if he's the one behind the arson, then we need to find him before someone gets hurt—or worse. And it looks like it's up to me to find enough evidence to convince the sheriff that we have a problem.

Game on.

6

RUSS

"When you said 'cabin,' this wasn't what I had in mind," Liam said, looking around as Russ ushered him inside.

"It might have been built to be a summer place originally, but over time my grandfather's friend added on to it, and then Drew and I did our own fixing up and made additions to make it a year-round home."

"It's nice. Cozy," Liam replied. "Snug in the winter?"

"Yeah. Good insulation and a heavy-duty furnace are necessities here," Russ replied, leading Liam into the kitchen and motioning him to a chair at the table. "I, uh, checked with Rich Jeffries about your bungalow furnace and insulation. You'll be just fine." He grinned. "I can't help what the weather is like outside. That will take some adjusting, compared to what you've been used to in Ithaca."

"Thank you." Liam looked surprised at the simple kindness, and a stab of protectiveness went through Russ to think that Liam found the gesture so unusual.

"I hope lasagna is okay," Russ said, glancing over his shoulder. "It's homemade. Drew and I try to cook and freeze meals, so we don't have to think about it much during the week."

"Lasagna sounds wonderful," Liam replied with enthusiasm. "I've gotten better at cooking, but there's still a long way to go. I do a lot of sandwiches for lunch, and I bought a slow cooker, so at least on some nights I have a hot dinner waiting when I get back."

It was all Russ could do not to invite Liam to move in.

He should be with his pack. We would make sure he eats well, his wolf argued.

Too soon. Let me handle this.

It would be good for us not to get old alone. His wolf trotted off.

Aren't you just a fucking ray of sunshine, Russ silently shouted after his other self.

"Russ?"

"Sorry," Russ said, realizing he'd spaced out. He managed a lopsided smile. "Does your fox ever get lippy with you?"

"All the freakin' time," Liam replied, laughing. "We have epic arguments, and I will warn you—he's dramatic."

"My wolf thinks he knows everything," Russ said. "We disagree."

"I take it he had an opinion?" Liam asked.

"He has opinions on everything." Russ pulled a loaf of garlic bread out of the freezer and put it on a baking sheet, then dumped a bag of salad into a bowl. "Most of the time, he's okay. He just doesn't understand that humans do things differently."

"I'm still getting used to being able to talk about this stuff," Liam admitted, accepting a beer when Russ popped the cap and handed him the bottle. "You're lucky to have a pack. I never had a skulk, so I had to figure it out as I went along."

"A skulk is a fox pack?" Russ asked without turning as he added extras to the salad—cheese, croutons.

"Yes. It was just my mother and me, and then she passed away."

"Sorry to hear that."

"It happens."

"Drew is my brother, but the other guys from the firehouse—Ty, Justin, and Brandon—they're not wolves, but they're pack," Russ said, not trusting himself to look back as he spoke. "More than the rest of my family ever was."

"I'm glad you found them."

Russ couldn't miss the wistfulness in Liam's voice. "There's always room for more," he said, wondering if his voice sounded as tight to Liam as it did to him.

"Good to know."

Russ sensed Liam's hesitation without needing to see him. "Whatever it is, you can tell me."

"I started to, last time, before your phone went off," Liam said. "There isn't a good way to say it, but it's something you need to know. About how I ended up here." He took a deep breath and let it out. "I'm pretty sure my ex hired a Huntsman to kill me."

A growl rose from Russ's throat as his wolf surged to the fore. "What happened?" He turned to see Liam, and the look of fear and uncertainty nearly broke Russ's heart.

"We broke up six months ago. Caught him cheating. Probably not the first time, but it was the last," Liam recounted, his voice going flat and toneless. "He stalked me. There were…incidents. I took out a restraining order. It just made him angrier. But then…nothing. I thought he went away. And then I got a call from a friend who heard him bragging that he'd put out a hit on me—with a Huntsman. I went out my window with what I could carry as a man with a gun came up the steps."

Russ gripped the edge of the counter white-knuckled, fighting to keep his wolf at bay. The thought that he'd nearly lost Liam before he ever found him made his blood run hot.

"Dr. Jeffries had offered me a job, out of the blue, just a couple of days before. Psychic, you know?" Liam said. "I called him from the road and accepted. And, here I am."

Russ closed the distance between them and pulled Liam into his arms, wrapping his body around him, tucking Liam's head beneath his chin. Liam only hesitated for a second before he leaned into the embrace, slipping his arms around Russ's waist.

"Where is he?" Russ's voice was a deep rumble.

Liam shook his head. "The Huntsman? I don't know. I doubt my ex, Kelson, could be bothered to leave Ithaca." He paused again, and from the way Liam tensed, Russ knew there was more to the story.

"I'm afraid that the fires and the missing hikers might be connected," Liam confided from the safety of Russ's embrace.

Russ's howl of sheer rage startled both of them. He tightened his arms around Liam, folding him snug against his body. "We're going to keep you safe," he promised. "I swear it."

Liam buried his face in Russ's shirt. "I don't want anyone else to get hurt."

"Don't worry about us. Did you tell the sheriff?"

Liam shook his head. "I told Dr. Jeffries. But I can't prove anything. The sheriff will want proof."

Much as Russ wanted to argue the point, he knew Liam was right. "Torben is a good guy, but he's by-the-book. You walk in talking about a Huntsman, and I'm not sure how that will go over."

"Do you believe me?"

"Yes. I'm your mate. I can smell the truth on you."

The oven timer went off, and Russ reluctantly released him, figuring that a good meal would go a long way toward soothing frayed nerves. He made their plates at the counter, focusing on nurturing and feeding his mate, trying to let go of his anger and protectiveness.

"There's more if you want it," Russ said, placing a plate in front of Liam.

Liam sniffed at the aroma wafting from the big slice of lasagna. "This smells wonderful. If you cook like this all the time, you might never get rid of me."

"I like the sound of that," Russ replied with a mischievous smile. Liam blushed but gave him a shy grin in return. Russ had the definite feeling that Liam was rarely shy, and he loved seeing a part of Liam that he didn't present to the whole world.

"One of these nights, we need to go to see something at the Saranac Theater," Russ said, looking for topics to lighten the mood. As grateful as he was that Liam shared his secret with him, Russ wanted to give him a good evening to forget his worries. "The theater itself is part of the show."

"We had a family-owned place like that in Ithaca," Liam replied. "There was always a bat in the building, and you never knew when it was going to swoop in front of the screen during the movie."

Russ laughed. "That must have been exciting, but that's not what I meant. The Saranac Theater was built in the 1920s, and for some reason the owner built all this paper mâché scenery around the edges of the stage—rocks and fake trees and logs—like we don't have enough nature around here. The walls have hand-painted murals, and there are these gargoyle-type carvings of local wildlife all along the balcony railing."

"I need to see that," Liam agreed, licking a bit of tomato sauce from his lip with a flick of that pink tongue. Russ shifted in his chair, overwhelmed with ideas about how he'd like to see that tongue in action.

"The Saranac plays movies, and it's also the site for live plays, for the community theater and the summer arts program," Russ replied. "And since the library plays a big role with that, I imagine you'll spend plenty of time there."

"Getting the youth programs to do mini-plays over the summer is one of my favorite things." The enthusiasm that filled Liam's tone made Russ smile. "I love to see the students come out of their shells. They're all afraid of looking silly at first, and by the end, they're into their roles with everything they've got."

"Were you in the drama program in school?" Russ could imagine Liam indulging his fox diva. Just seeing Liam light up with excitement was enough for Russ.

Liam shrugged. "Not as much as I would have liked. I had to keep my grades up to qualify for scholarships, but the little bit I was involved, I liked. That's another reason I love to offer a drama program over the summer, so everyone can be involved."

"I like going to plays, although I never had the desire to be up on stage. But if you are, I'll be your number one fan." Russ reached over to lay his hand over Liam's.

"I'll hold you to that," Liam replied. "You know, I think the biggest thing I learned—and what I see a lot of the students come away with— is that you can be scared to do something, and if you pretend you're playing a character who's brave, you can be brave too."

Russ kept the conversation light throughout dinner, trading funny stories and comparing notes on movies and TV shows. He could see Liam relaxing and felt his wolf's approval.

When dinner was over, Liam offered to lend a hand as Russ cleared the table. "Let me help," Liam said. "That way, it's done, and you don't have to think about it again."

Russ didn't try to argue. He liked maneuvering around Liam in the cabin's kitchen, working in sync as if they'd been doing this for years. *Like Liam belongs here.*

Liam dried his hands as he finished the last of the dishes. Russ came up behind him and slipped his arms around Liam's waist, snuggling close behind him. Liam leaned back against him, letting his head fall against Russ's chest. Russ shifted his hips so that his erection slotted between the firm cheeks of Liam's ass.

"I've been hard for you all the way through dinner," Russ murmured, bending his head to breathe in Liam's scent, loving the shiver that went through Liam's whole body. "I want to make you feel good."

"I like feeling good." Liam's voice had gone breathy, and he pushed back against Russ, leaving no question about his interest.

Russ turned Liam in his arms, and kissed him, starting with his lips, then both eyelids, his cheekbones, nose, and chin. He cupped his hand around Liam's prominent bulge, and let his thumb stroke down the hard line.

"I want to taste you." Russ's voice had become a low growl. "That okay?"

"Yes," Liam's voice had changed pitch, a bit more of a yip. "Please, Russ."

Russ dropped to his knees, and nosed along Liam's groin through his jeans, running his hands down strong thighs and then around to give that pert ass a good squeeze. He unbuckled Liam's belt and tugged his zipper open before pushing the jeans down to his ankles.

Liam's stiff cock strained against the fabric of his briefs, which were already damp with evidence of his arousal. Russ inhaled Liam's scent, rubbing his cheek against the cloth, then mouthing his way up Liam's prick from bottom to top, breathing out through his mouth in warm puffs that made Liam buck and wriggle.

"Want you, Russ."

Russ hooked his thumbs in the waistband and pulled down, exposing his mate's fine package. The last time they'd been together,

Russ had gotten to touch, but he didn't get a good view. Now, he could look all he wanted, taking in the elegant, slim length, the uncut tip, and the nest of russet hair.

He pushed his face against Liam, as a low rumble in his throat made his desire clear. He gripped Liam's hips, holding him in place, firm but not tightly enough to bruise, although the idea of marking his mate had a visceral appeal.

"I love your scent." Russ kissed the cleft of Liam's groin before making his way over to the beautiful shaft, then going lower, to lick at his balls and suck each one into his mouth, rolling them on his tongue.

"Oh God, Russ," Liam moaned, sinking his hands into Russ's hair.

Russ released Liam's balls and licked his way up Liam's cock with the flat of his tongue, then swirled around the head, tasting his pre-come, making sure to press the tip into his sensitive slit. Russ bobbed up, and this time he swallowed Liam down in one move, taking him to the root. He moaned as the knob of Liam's cock hit the back of his throat.

"Holy shit," Liam yelped, hips bucking. Russ held him in place, rising and then sinking down again. He hummed as he hollowed his cheeks, loving the sounds that vibration drew from Liam, relishing the chance to give his mate pleasure.

He let his tongue stroke the velvet length, tracing the vein, swirling and lapping until all Liam could do was moan.

"Russ...I'm gonna—" Liam tried to pull back, but Russ held on and added the slight scrape of teeth. A second later, Liam's warm load shot down his throat, and Russ swallowed it, relishing his taste. He took it all, then lapped at the head of Liam's over-sensitive cock to get the very last drops.

He looked up and nearly lost it at the sight of Liam's flushed cheeks, lust-blown pupils, and open mouth, feeling proud to have put that look on his mate's face. Russ kissed the tip of Liam's softened dick, loving the way that made his partner shiver.

"That was...amazing," Liam managed, breathless.

Russ rose to his feet and took Liam in his arms, sharing a taste with him as he pressed their mouths together.

"My turn," Liam whispered, running his hands down Russ's chest as he knelt in front of him. Liam made short work of Russ's belt and jeans, shoving down his underwear with the denim, and pausing for a good look. The naked want in Liam's eyes thrilled Russ on a gut level.

My mate is pleased.

Russ's cock was thicker than Liam's, though they were close to the same length. Liam worked one hand between Russ's legs and cupped his ass with the other. Russ groaned as Liam's fingers stroked his taint, while his tongue flicked up his hard length, teasing and tasting.

"So damn sexy," Liam murmured. He looked up at Russ from beneath pale lashes, meeting his gaze as Liam fastened his lips over the head of Russ's cock at the same moment one finger traced the rim of his hole.

"Not gonna last long if you keep that up," Russ breathed, so turned on he felt weak in the knees. He tangled his fingers in Liam's red hair, tugging gently and hearing a pleased moan in response.

"Uh-humm." Liam sank down on Russ's shaft. He stroked Russ's pucker again, then tugged gently on his balls. He wrapped his hand around the root of Russ's cock and went down on him in earnest until Russ trembled all over and his body stiffened.

Russ cried out Liam's name, shooting down his throat and filling his mouth until a dribble of his come slipped from the corner of Liam's lips.

Liam looked up at him again, smiling around Russ's cock, a glint of pride and possession in his tilted amber eyes.

Russ gently lifted Liam to face him, licking away the drops of jizz on his lover's chin and lips, then kissing him with tender fervor. It was far too soon to say everything that filled his heart. Russ knew that he and Liam were finding their way toward each other, and he now understood that the betrayal Liam had suffered made him understandably wary.

I'll wait. I'll prove myself, day by day, until you believe, with no doubt. You're worth it.

"Stay the night," Russ whispered, relishing how it felt to hold Liam in his arms.

"I need to open the library by nine," Liam replied, resting his forehead on Russ's chest.

"I have to open the auto shop at eight, so I'll have you home in plenty of time to grab a change of clothing."

"You say all the right things," Liam teased, running his hands up and down Russ's back.

"So, yes?" Russ found he was holding his breath.

Liam chuckled. "Yes."

They curled up together on the couch to watch a movie, increasingly comfortable in each other's space. Russ loved having Liam pressed against him, running his hands through Liam's soft hair. Liam shifted to leave no room between them, making it clear that he liked the arrangement.

"Isn't Drew coming home?" Liam asked after a while, as if he had just remembered that Russ shared the cabin.

Russ chuckled. "He and Ty were planning an all-night gaming marathon. He won't be home until about the time we need to leave."

Reassured that they didn't have to worry about interruptions, Liam settled back against Russ, sated and sleepy.

Our mate is satisfied, Russ's wolf said.

I certainly hope so.

We are extremely compatible. The wolf sounded smug.

I am not discussing that with you, Russ replied, wishing that for once his wolf would mind his own business.

I was there.

Eww. Just, TMI dude. I do not want to think about you riding shotgun when we're…just, no.

He is our mate.

Go away.

When the movie ended, Liam turned in Russ's arms, planting kisses on his cheek, then lower to his jaw and lower still to lick and nibble at the base of his neck along his pulse point. Russ returned the kisses, and felt his body respond, wanting more. He didn't want to push Liam for more than he was comfortable doing, but his body ached for them to take their connection to the next level.

Liam shifted, pressing his erection against Russ's thigh. "I want to feel you in me," he whispered and slid his hand between Russ's legs. "If you want to."

Russ growled as he claimed Liam's mouth. "Oh, I want to." He sucked on Liam's bottom lip and added a gentle scrape of teeth that sent a shiver through Liam's entire body. Liam sucked on Russ's tongue, doing wonderful, erotic things with the flicking of his own tongue against the captured flesh, making promises about what he would like to do with Russ's cock.

Liam stripped out of his shirt and dropped it on the floor. He pushed his hands under Russ's shirt, and Russ happily accommodated him, yanking it over his head and adding it to the pile. Jeans and underwear came off in a hurried slide until they were finally both naked.

Russ licked his lips, taking in the gorgeous man in front of him. A dusting of cinnamon hair covered Liam's pale skin, darker where a ginger happy trail led to his very hard cock. Russ ran his hands down Liam's chest, appreciating the toned body and lean muscles.

Liam chuckled. "The way you're licking your lips makes me feel like Little Red Riding Hood."

"Oh, Red, I will be glad to be your big, bad wolf," Russ teased, raking Liam with an appreciative gaze that sent an adorable blush to the other man's ears.

"And I'd like to be riding you, so it sounds like we're both in the right story," Liam replied with a flirty wink.

Russ shifted, giving Liam a better view of his own painfully stiff dick. Liam traced Russ's muscles, from his defined pecs down washboard abs. Russ had more body scruff, brown and gray like his hair, which he tried to tame with some careful manscaping. From the way Liam petted him, Russ got the idea that his partner didn't mind at all.

He moved forward and kissed Liam on the lips. "You're sure about this? No pressure."

Liam nodded, although Russ thought he still looked a little nervous. "Yes. Except…maybe we can wait a little bit on the biting part? I want to… I just need to get my nerve up for that."

Russ hushed his wolf, who was eager to mark and claim. "There's no rush. Whatever you want, when you want it."

A mischievous gleam came into Liam's eyes, making them more

like the amber of his fox. He reached down between them and gave Russ's ample cock a tug. "I want you."

"How do you want to do it?"

Liam got up and walked around the couch. Then he leaned onto his forearms, pressing them against the back of the couch, while he spread his legs wide and offered up his pert ass. "Will this do?" he asked, feigning innocence.

"Oh, I'll do you real good like that," Russ promised. "Let me grab stuff. I'll be right back."

He returned with lube and paused to take in the perfect image of Liam shamelessly putting himself on display. His cock managed to get even harder, balls already heavy and aching.

Russ came to stand behind Liam and bent to kiss down the rise of his spine. He rubbed against Liam's ass and thighs, close enough that his rough body hair promised a delicious burn. Liam shimmied back against him, and Russ thought he was going to lose it right then.

"Um, I don't know if you know that shifters don't get STDs like humans," Russ said.

"I picked up one of the 'learning about your shifter self' books out of the library and skipped to the good parts," Liam admitted. "My education was a bit thin on that side of things. But, thank you. And... I'm ready to feel you." He waggled his hips, just to make his point clear.

Russ slicked up one hand and reached around to grip Liam's cock and began to stroke slowly while he spread Liam's cheeks wide with the other and started to lick down his crack. Liam groaned, and his entire body trembled, giving Russ the idea he was on the right track.

"Oh, God. Is that rimming? Fuck, that feels amazing. I might not make it to the main event. Holy shit!"

Russ chuckled as he kept exploring, loving the sounds he drew from his lover as the tip of his tongue traced the rim of Liam's tight rosette. He nosed lower, losing himself in the scent of Liam's intimate musk, sliding the flat of his tongue along the taint, and gently sucking on one of his balls and then the other.

Liam thrust back against him and then fucked forward into his fist, making desperate little noises in his throat. A sheen of sweat covered

Liam's skin. From Liam's reactions, Russ guessed that his past partners hadn't taken much time for niceties. That was fine with Russ, whose wolf growled at the thought of Liam being with anyone else. He resolved to spend forever teaching Liam what he knew of pleasure and exploring new possibilities together.

Russ returned his attention to Liam's tight pucker. He poked at it with his furled tongue, alternating with licking around the rim to help loosen him. Then he stopped stroking Liam just long enough to slick up the fingers on his other hand, and returned to his slow strokes while one finger worked its way inside.

"Christ, Russ! I'm not gonna last. Do me now, please!"

"Want this to be good for you," Russ said and gave a light nip to Liam's ass cheek, which got a yelp and a shimmy in response. He hadn't broken the skin or left a mark, but he felt a primal satisfaction.

Russ shifted on his knees for a better angle, and added a second finger, while he kissed along Liam's lower back. He fastened his mouth on one spot just above his hipbone and began to suck a hickey as his fingers stretched Liam's tight hole, and his other hand provided a slick channel for Liam to fuck.

"That's it. Mark me," Liam panted. "Show me I'm yours."

Russ twisted his fingers, brushing across Liam's spot, and his lover arched, thrusting back against him. He pushed a third finger in to stretch Liam while he ran the flat of his tongue over the livid bruise of the hickey, proud to leave proof of their union.

"Want to come with you inside me," Liam said in a breathy voice. "C'mon, Russ. Fuck me now."

Russ cracked open the lube one-handed and slicked up his cock, so aroused he feared for a second he might lose it just from that scant friction. He gripped Liam's hip with one hand, still stroking his cock with the other, and pressed against his hole, which still resisted entry despite all his foreplay.

"Just do it," Liam moaned. Russ pushed in partway, then stilled, giving Liam time to adjust. He knew despite his prep that it had to hurt a little and felt Liam's erection flag. Russ drew back a bit, stroking Liam back to hardness, letting him relax around the girth of the cock in his ass. When he sensed Liam was ready, he worked his way inside, slow strokes to minimize the stretch and burn, and finally seated himself fully, balls-deep. Russ needed to take a moment so he didn't blow his load right then from the tight heat that gripped him and pulled him in.

Liam shoved back against him, a clear signal to get moving. Russ gave a throaty laugh in response and pulled back, then slid home again, beginning a rhythm that soon had him sweaty and gasping. He knew he wasn't going to last long.

All of that drove him close to the edge, along with something inde-finably *more*. Every sensation felt like it had been turned up to maxi-mum, exploding through his senses. The sound of Liam's moans and his own stuttered breathing, the smell of mingled sweat and the last round's come, the taste of Liam's skin on his lips. All of it was almost too much, and simultaneously not yet quite enough.

Russ stroked Liam's cock faster and felt Liam go rigid beneath him as his orgasm hit, drawing out a howl of ecstasy. That drove Russ over the brink, and he pounded Liam's ass with short, hard strokes as he chased his release. For an instant, Russ swore he could feel Liam's bliss *from the inside*, experiencing his lover's emotions as his own. He nearly whited out at the intensity of his climax, so that at the end, he and Liam's combined weight was being supported by the couch as they both went weak in the knees.

Shaking, he drew Liam down with him, still connected, and wrapped his arms around Liam's chest. Liam let his head fall back, exposing that beautiful expanse of throat, and it took all of Russ's willpower not to bite like his wolf demanded.

Instead, he kissed and licked a trail from chin to shoulder, and then buried his face in Liam's red hair when he no longer trusted himself to behave.

"I love you," he whispered next to Liam's ear. "Mate."

"Umm," Liam murmured dreamily, thoroughly sated. "Love you too, mate."

If Russ had harbored any remaining doubts about whether he and Liam were fated mates, their joining banished those thoughts. Nothing in his life prepared him for the intensity of their union, or that instant of shared consciousness, of being Russ-and-Liam without barriers, truly one in body, mind, and soul.

Liam seemed content to lie bonelessly in Russ's embrace, even as Russ's cock slipped out, followed by a trickle of come. Russ wished they could stay like that forever, wrapped up completely in each other. But he realized Liam's skin had begun to prickle with goosebumps, and he knew that if they didn't clean up, they would regret it come morning.

"What...where?" Liam managed as Russ pushed to his feet, carrying Liam in his arms.

"I'm taking you to bed," Russ replied, voice low and gravelly. "Gonna clean us up, so we're not a mess in the morning. And I'm going to hold you all night long."

Liam made a sexy murmur of assent. "I like that. A lot."

Russ set him down gently on the bed, then went into the bathroom and returned with a wet washcloth to wipe up both of them, then tossed the cloth in the clothes bin. He'd clean off the back of the couch tomorrow where Liam's come had spattered against it. Liam watched him with a sleepy gaze, eyes wide and vulnerable, walls down. Russ wondered what Liam saw in his own eyes, and if he was equally open.

He didn't know how to ask whether Liam had felt that zing of extra connection, afraid to discover it might have been all in his imagination.

"That was...different," Liam murmured, sounding sleep-slurred as he shifted to lay his head on Russ's shoulder. "For a minute there, I was kinda you but still me. Both. Maybe?" His gaze searched Russ's eyes, seeking validation.

Russ swallowed hard and nodded. "Yeah. Me too. I think it's part of the fated mates thing. Probably where the whole 'soulmates' thing comes from." His heart leaped, thinking that might be true.

"That's good," Liam replied, so quietly Russ could barely hear him. He pressed a kiss to Liam's temple.

"Very, very good, my sexy fox."

"Big bad wolfie." Liam's voice drifted off before Russ could object to the nickname.

Wolfie, huh. I kinda like that.

Russ's wolf gave a huff. *Certainly not.*

Oh, lighten up. He just fucked my brains out. If he wants to call me Wolfie, I'm not going to complain about it.

Perhaps it will be tolerable, his wolf allowed. *Since he is our mate.*

Fated mate.

Assuredly so.

Russ fell asleep with Liam tucked close to his side. Liam's head was on Russ's shoulder. Their scents mingled with the smell of sex and sweat, and Russ wondered how long he would need to hold off on finishing their bond.

We've barely known each other for a week. That's a little soon for "move in with me" and "let me seal this with a bite."

His wolf gave a disdainful sniff. *Too quick for humans. Not for shifters. We are fated mates. What more is there to discuss?*

Russ lay awake, listening to Liam breathe. He hadn't been with anyone since Anthony died, and he had become numb to sleeping alone. For the first year after he'd been widowed, Russ had taken comfort in the bed that used to be theirs, imagining that he could still pick up traces of Anthony's scent, as if the mattress held more than memories. Last year, in an optimistic declaration that he was going to "move on," Russ had bought a new mattress and all-new bedding.

Nothing had changed.

Now, he felt glad that this bed was unburdened by memories, and that it could be *their* bed, his and Liam's. As hard as it had been to finally give away or box up Anthony's belongings, except for a few cherished items, Russ realized that doing so had freed up space in his home, life, and heart to love again.

He waited to feel guilty like he was a bad husband and a faithless lover. Instead, a sense of peace mantled around him.

That night, he dreamed of walking on a beach with Anthony, hand in hand, something they had never actually done but talked about doing in a someday vacation. For a while, they walked in silence, broken only by the rushing waves and the gulls overhead. They turned to watch the ocean as the water lapped against their bare feet.

"You'll be okay," dream-Anthony said quietly, looking out across the water.

"I don't think I'll ever be okay again without you," dream-Russ replied.

Anthony turned and smiled at him, that amazing grin that had made Russ fall head-over-heels. "Then remember me, remember us...but don't let it hold you back from living. I'd stay if I could. But I can't. So when you find someone, know you have my blessing."

The wind from the ocean stung Russ's eyes, and he blinked to clear them.

Anthony was gone.

Russ woke to the sound of the alarm signal on his phone. Liam startled, looking momentarily panicked, waking in an unfamiliar place.

"Shh, you're safe," Russ soothed. "It's my phone."

"There's another fire?"

"Yeah, probably." Russ grabbed his phone and saw that it was just after five in the morning. He listened to the message and swore under his breath.

"I've got to go in. There's a blaze. I swear, things aren't normally like this. I've been with the department for ten years, and I've never seen it like this before."

He leaned down to kiss Liam, who still looked adorably sleepy. "Come on, I'll drive you home. Believe me, this isn't how I wanted our morning to go."

Liam reached up to cup the back of Russ's head, lengthening the kiss for a few more seconds. He drew back and looked into Russ's eyes. "Be careful. Please."

"Always."

They dressed quickly, and Russ followed Liam out of the door and into the cold pre-dawn morning, locking up behind them. "Sorry about this," he said, disappointed at the rushed end to their date.

"It's okay," Liam assured him. "I had a friend in Ithaca who was dating a doctor. Same kind of thing happened. It goes with the territory. Just remember what I told you. Take extra precautions."

Russ's heart warmed at the concern in Liam's voice, and his easy acceptance of the interruption. "I'll take a raincheck on waking up with you when we can do it right," he said as they got into his car.

"I like that idea."

Few cars were on the street at this hour, but as they neared the center of town, Russ heard the fire sirens. He drove past the station and into the driveway to Liam's house, saying another hurried goodbye with a quick kiss and watching until Liam entered the bungalow, wary of having Liam walk home in the darkness with a Huntsman on the loose. Then he headed to the firehouse and walked right into the heart of the storm.

───────────

"WHAT HAPPENED?" Russ woke slowly, surfacing into pain. His throat and nasal passages felt raw, and his eyes stung so badly he slammed them shut as soon as they opened. The low beep and hum of machinery told him he was in a hospital, as if even his damaged nose couldn't smell the antiseptic.

"A beam came down," Drew said from his bedside. "Justin would have been right under it. You tackled him, and it mostly missed you both."

"Mostly?" Russ's voice sounded like he had gargled glass, and felt like it too.

"A lot of flaming crap fell with it, damaged your helmet, which is why the smoke got to you. It took us a bit to figure out how to get you out of there without having the whole place come down around our ears."

"How bad?" Russ managed. Drew held a Styrofoam cup with a straw for Russ to drink. The ice water soothed his throat.

"They want to hold you overnight for observation. Smoke inhalation. You'll have some spectacular technicolor bruises from where debris hit, but your suit protected you. If you weren't a shifter, you'd be a lot worse."

Fox Hollow had its own hospital since shifters and those with supernatural abilities could hardly go to a regular facility. Thanks to generous funding from the community and the Institute, the hospital had everything necessary to handle even critical cases.

"Justin?"

"Not quite as lucky," Drew admitted, replacing the cup on the nightstand when Russ waved it away. "He's going to be okay," he said quickly, holding up a hand to still Russ. "But he landed hard and fucked up his knee. He's in surgery. I talked to Ty's mom—she's Justin's emergency contact, since he doesn't have family around here. She told me the doctor said they think they can fix it, but it'll be a long recovery, and he might be off the truck for good, depending on how it heals."

"Fuck."

"Yeah," Drew replied. "But it's still better than what would have happened if the beam had fallen differently. Dammit, Russ, we could have lost both of you."

Firefighting was dangerous work. Everyone who put on a turnout suit knew that. Drills and training repeated that truth, so no one grew complacent. Still, Russ had ten years without a serious injury, so he should have figured his luck would run out at some point.

"Liam?"

"I called him once the nurses got you settled. He's been here the whole time until about an hour ago when I made him leave to get some food, sleep, and a shower. If you don't think he already knows you're his mate, you're blind." Drew's expression grew wistful.

"Dude, I'm a little jealous," Drew continued. "You might not have been true mates with Anthony, but what you had was good. And now, you've found your fated mate. I sure hope there's someone like that, just one someone, out there for me."

"There is," Russ said, trying to reassure his little brother despite his own condition. He paused. Something Drew said puzzled him.

"Wait…the *whole time*?"

Russ remembered being in the downstairs of the burning two-story chalet-style summer house. He and Justin had gone in because the caller had said there were people and pets inside. That hadn't been true—or they had already fled. Russ had signaled to Justin that they needed to get out. The fire was gaining ground, burning hot, with more smoke than usual.

Just as Justin started toward Russ and the front door, Russ heard a loud crack. Instinct and experience warned him that one of the ceiling beams holding up the loft was going to give way, and he dove for Justin at the last second, sending them both to the floor. He didn't remember anything clearly after that.

"It's been twenty-four hours," Drew said, and Russ heard the exhaustion in his voice. "The doctors wanted to monitor you because of the smoke—to check for carbon monoxide poisoning and potential cyanide exposure. We weren't sure whether there was anything else toxic that burned, or how badly the smoke might have affected your lungs. Plus, they wanted to keep an eye on your heart. They had to give you a sedative for some of the tests, so you've been in and out. Justin's in surgery, and they're keeping him for observation, although he didn't get the dose of smoke you did."

"I feel like a house fell on me."

Drew's expression tightened. "Don't joke. It nearly did. We barely got the two of you out before the whole thing came down."

As craptastic as Russ felt, he knew what Drew said didn't sound right. "That shouldn't have happened."

"No shit, Sherlock," his brother replied. "Cap's there with the sheriff, and the forensic team they brought in from Plattsburgh. He called to check on you. Says that it's not only looking like arson, but he thinks someone weakened key support beams and may have tossed some bad burnables into the mix just to make the smoke more dangerous."

Russ's mind felt like a computer struggling to download with a lousy signal. The information he needed felt just out of reach. Finally, his thoughts cleared enough for him to remember what he had to tell Drew.

"Liam's in danger," he rasped. "Make sure the sheriff talks to him. I think he's on to something."

Drew frowned, looking at Russ as if he might be hallucinating. Russ shook his head, struggling to make himself clear. He reached out to grab Drew's wrist, dragging his IV line across the sheet.

"Rich Jeffries knows—Liam told him. Talk to them. Urgent."

Drew seemed to find what he needed to assure himself that Russ was lucid and nodded. "Okay."

Russ didn't let go as memories filtered back. "Protect him. Don't let him do something stupid."

Drew's eyes narrowed. "Like what?"

"Run. Or fight."

Drew looked like he wanted to ask more questions, but Russ had already pushed himself as far as he could go. His brother gave him a disapproving glare. "I'll go find Liam, and see when I can get the sheriff here. You okay without me for a little bit?"

Russ nodded and made a shooing motion. He still felt groggy from the smoke and the medication, but he was aware enough to be worried for his mate.

This is exactly what Liam was afraid would happen if a Huntsman was behind it. He's either going to run away "for my own good" or try to settle the score himself. Either way, I could lose my mate before he's finally mine.

7

LIAM

THIS IS ALL MY FAULT.

Liam closed the door of the house behind him and turned the lock, then fell back against the wood with a gasp. The tears he fought back at Russ's bedside spilled over, and Liam felt too heartsick to try to keep them inside any longer.

If he still had any question about whether his connection to Russ was real, the way his heart nearly stopped when Drew called him put all doubts to rest.

Mate. Skulk. Mine.

For once, man and fox were in complete agreement. Liam pushed his penchant for dramatics aside and focused on the cunning and stubbornness for which foxes were known, and the wrathfulness of his Leo nature.

I could run, but now that the Huntsman has found Fox Hollow, there's nothing to keep him from coming back after he chases me. No one's found those two missing hikers. And I don't want to leave Russ.

He had left the library as soon as Drew called, with Linda and Maddi promising to take care of everything and urging him to go to Russ. He'd arrived to find Drew waiting for him, looking worried and scared. Liam had listened as Drew told him what had happened at the chalet, confirming his worst fears.

The arsonist had stepped up his game. Liam felt more sure than ever that the fire-setter either was the Huntsman or was working with him. What other explanation could there be? Whether he'd intentionally targeted Russ because of Liam, or just meant to cause as much chaos and injury as possible to first responders as a distraction, Liam wasn't sure. But if he was right about his ex having set the Huntsman on him, then targeting Liam's new lover wouldn't be a stretch.

Russ had been groggy with pain medications and sedatives when Liam arrived. Despite the hospital's efforts to clean him up enough to treat his injuries, the smell of the fire permeated everything. Drew told Liam that it didn't smell like a campfire because when a house burned so many other flammables also ignited, and that made it stink of plastic, varnish, and so much more.

Liam pushed a chair up beside Russ's bed and took his hand, as Drew went to get food and clean up. Nurses stopped in to check on Russ, but Liam knew they wouldn't tell him anything. Couldn't. Because right now, Liam was technically nothing to Russ, legally speaking. Human laws didn't recognize shifter mates, and their relationship was so new that there had been no time to formalize anything.

Hell, we're still blundering around like idiots ourselves, Liam thought. Even so, Drew must have said something to the shift nurse because no one quibbled with Liam staying past visiting hours. Drew had come back, bringing Liam coffee and a sandwich, then briefed him on Russ's condition once he'd talked to the doctor.

He'll live. He'll probably be okay, but it was close. Too close.

"I'm here," Liam murmured, leaning close to Russ's ear. "I'm not going anywhere. I'm so sorry. This is my fault."

He thought he felt Russ's fingers tighten around his hand, a weak squeeze.

"We'll find him. The arsonist. We'll make him pay. I promise you." Liam bent his head and lifted Russ's hand to kiss his knuckles.

"You're right about us being fated mates. It's soon and it's fast and it's scary, but come back to me, and we'll figure it out. Together. Just…don't go."

Over the course of long hours, Liam kept up a running one-sided conversation, talking about anything and everything just to break the silence. He told Russ about the plans he and Maddi and Linda were making for the summer in excruciating detail, as well as what he had learned about the gaps in his predecessor's record-keeping toward the end, and some of the holes they would need to fix in the library's acquisitions.

When he ran out of library stories, he recounted interesting anecdotes about his time at Ithaca, told every joke he could remember, and fanboyed over his favorite books and movies. Gradually, Russ stirred, waking up, coming back to Liam as he had begged him to do.

Liam had felt a surge of relief at seeing Russ's eyes open, a feeling so strong it made him light-headed. He hadn't been surprised when Russ faded quickly, but Liam had been glad that Russ was safe and getting the care he needed. Even shifters weren't indestructible.

Once Liam felt sure Russ was out of danger, he knew he needed to act. The sheriff and the fire chief were tied up with the arson investigation, and Liam didn't have any hard proof—just a bunch of far-fetched suspicions.

He had wracked his brain on how to find real evidence, something that they could use to shut down the Huntsman and hopefully find the missing hikers before it was too late. Liam didn't know the trails, and after the search parties combed the area and found nothing, he concluded that the Huntsman had either removed his prisoners immediately or had a hideout remote enough to evade notice. The forest was too vast for Liam to think he might stumble upon the Huntsman's bolt hole.

But the locals might know.

Liam had been on the lookout for other non-shifter foxes since he arrived, figuring that he should introduce himself, although his previous experience with his wild neighbors was somewhat uneven.

In Ithaca, the quasi-domesticated foxes that frequented suburban neighborhoods had reacted to Liam as if he were a savage threat. Those out in the actual forest regarded him with curiosity and a whiff of disdain, as if his dual nature diluted his foxhood, or worse, made him a pet. A few were able to overcome their reservations, and those became good relationships that helped Liam understand missing pieces about the fox side of himself no one had bothered to explain.

From the search party information, Liam knew where the hikers went missing. He bustled around the bungalow, gathering items he thought he might need, trying to predict a variety of possible outcomes. He had hoped that he and Russ could have gone snooping in their fur together, but Russ was going to be sidelined for a while, and the men had already been missing for several days.

Still, it seemed foolhardy to go alone. Liam debated the issue with himself and finally texted Dr. Jeffries, hoping his mentor would understand.

Liam: Want to know if the local foxes have seen anything that might help find those hikers. Going to nose around and see what I can learn. Plan to be back in a few hours. If not, please come looking. I'm leaving my phone with its GPS finder Tile in my car, and I'll find a way to carry one of the Tiles with me. Here's how to locate me.

He included the log-in for his app and ended with the coordinates of the trail he intended to explore.

As he pulled out of the driveway, Liam wondered if the police had already tried interviewing the wildlife, since the sheriff was a shifter. Then again, bears tended to intimidate other creatures. Foxes were predators, but the mid-sized and larger animals didn't perceive them to be the same level of threat as a wolf or a bear. If he got lucky and found a native fox or two, they might be able to answer his questions without the need to try to communicate with any other type of animal.

He parked at the trailhead, surprised to find the lot fairly empty. He reminded himself that since it was mid-afternoon, many hikers might have gotten an early start and already gone home. Liam had plans to eat dinner with Russ at the hospital and fill him in on his news, so he intended to do a little investigating and then head back.

Liam sized up his options for shifting. Although the lot was quiet now, it would be just his luck to leave his clothes beneath his car and come back to find the local teenagers having a kegger. Instead, he slipped behind the primitive restroom at the edge of the lot and stripped quickly, and tucked his rolled-up clothing into a corner where he hoped it would go unnoticed. He took the GPS tracker Tile out of his pocket and placed it on the ground.

He shifted and then sniffed the air, getting his bearings. Liam gently picked up the tracker Tile and hoped that holding it in his mouth wouldn't completely shut it down. Liam knew the device had a limited range, but it was the best he could do with what he had on hand.

The area wasn't familiar, but Liam wasn't afraid of getting lost. The same sensitivity to the earth's magnetic core that aided his hunting also provided an inborn compass.

One thing that had bothered Liam about the two missing shifter-hikers was that there was no way they just "got lost." He could well imagine humans losing their way in the vast, rugged Adirondack forest. It wasn't completely impossible to imagine that the two men might have been injured or killed by a fall, an attack by a wild animal, or even a frightened camper with a gun. But if any of those scenarios had occurred, Liam felt sure the details would have surfaced by now. Everyone spoke well of Sheriff Armel, so he doubted incompetence was the issue.

Finding someone who wanted to be found could be challenging. Finding someone who was actively trying to hide—like the Huntsman —added a whole new level of difficulty.

First, Liam needed to find the foxes. Liam followed his nose, focusing on the musky scent. He left the trail—easy on all fours and in a form better suited to travel through the tangled brush. Liam knew he might not find many foxes, but if he could just talk to a few, he might learn something, or at the least, persuade them to keep a sharp lookout and provide updates.

He hadn't wandered far before he caught a stronger whiff, navigating the rocky ground and hopping over tree roots, footing that was treacherous for humans.

A warning bark and hiss revealed a male fox blocking his path, defending his territory. Liam had found a skulk, but he had no desire to fight.

Here's where it could get interesting, Liam thought. He mentally spoke with his shifter self in human language, aided by images and flashes of feelings. Wild foxes had a complex set of vocalizations, as well as body language, which they used to communicate. Liam was not a native speaker, despite his fur. Since he hadn't grown up with a skulk, and his mother had rarely shifted, his vocabulary was, at best, simple.

And I've probably got a funny accent.

Liam wagged his tail to show non-aggression. He cobbled his question together as best he could, feeling like a tourist with a bad phrase dictionary.

The barks, yips, and howls he strung together taxed his memory and his vocal cords. He hoped he had said, "Big strange cats go lost. Bad hunter maybe take? You see? Know?" Keeping the Tile in his mouth gave him a lisp, on top of everything else.

This is going to be like in those movies where I've accidentally insulted his honor and called his mother a hamster.

Two other foxes padded up behind the first one, all keeping their distance from Liam. He heard a muted back and forth in whines and growls but lacked the proficiency to guess what was being communicated.

Liam waited, increasingly uncomfortable with the stark evidence of just how far he was from being a wild animal. He could easily smell the native fox musk and the pungent aroma of their scent marking. *I probably smell like shampoo.*

The male fox brought his attention back to Liam. Liam desperately hoped he wouldn't be even more embarrassed by not understanding the answer.

To his relief, the male's string of chirps and yips was slow and simple enough to follow, as if he had guessed Liam's limited ability. What he picked up translated to, "Bad man, cage cats. Traps. Also kill ours."

Liam hadn't expected to learn that the Huntsman had also killed regular foxes. *One pelt is the same as another, I guess,* he thought, and shivered.

"Soon go."

Liam looked up. "You want I leave?" he managed in broken "foxish."

The male fox swished his tail in irritation. "No. He go. Soon. Take cats."

If it was the Huntsman, then he was either planning to make his move on Liam in the very near future or come back after he found a buyer for the cat-hikers. Either way, Liam's chance to find the Huntsman…and very possibly, the arsonist who nearly cost Russ his life… was closing fast.

"Show me where?" Liam asked before he had a chance to lose his nerve. "I stop him."

The male gave him a skeptical look. "Just you?"

Liam shook his head. "I bring friends."

Once again, the skulk conferred. Finally, the male turned back to Liam. "Follow."

The other foxes did not accompany them. If the Huntsman had already killed some of their group, Liam didn't blame them. He argued with himself the whole way, even as he did his best to remember the path so he could bring help back with him.

Not too smart to walk right up to the secret hideout of the guy who wants to kill me.

But there's no guarantee I'd meet up with these foxes again. And if they know where to find him—

Can't go back for a posse if I'm dead.

Can't bring in the cavalry if I don't know where the secret hideout is.

By this time, Liam figured they were more than half an hour off the trail, deep in the forest interior. Park visitors weren't supposed to leave the marked paths, for good reason. The stony ground made for treacherous footing. Rocky outcroppings that dropped off to deep ravines weren't uncommon.

Had the hiker who fell been running from someone? A shifter wouldn't hesitate to leave the regular trail, counting on instinct to find the way back. That same kind of awareness usually kept wild animals from plunging off cliffs by accident.

Unless he'd been running for his life. Or would have rather died than captured.

The male fox stopped abruptly, and Liam strained to make out his quiet chirps. "Ahead. Not far. Danger. I go. You come."

Liam did his best to fix the location in his mind so that he could lead the others back to free the cat-shifters. He fought the desire to get a look at the hideout, not wanting to test his luck. A quick nod signaled his agreement with his guide, who immediately turned and led them back the way they came, moving fast.

They were halfway back when Liam heard an odd zing, and then a sharp prick in his shoulder. He yipped, but the male fox doubled his pace and sprinted on, leaving Liam wobbling on his feet, suddenly dazed and losing control.

Fuck. I bet I've been tranqued, he thought as he fell over, awake and aware but unable to move.

A man stepped out of the underbrush, and Liam thought he matched the body shape of the person he'd seen set fire to the lake house. Instead of bike leathers, he wore canvas pants, a faded flannel shirt, and a heavy jacket. A wild mane of curly dark hair framed a broad, bearded face with piercing dark eyes.

"Well, well. If it's not the little fox shifter. You saved me another trip to town. I was trying to figure out what to burn next."

Liam's heart beat wildly. *How can he tell I'm a shifter? There's got to be some kind of magic involved.*

"I hope you don't expect your psychic pals to find you," the Huntsman said, reaching down to grab Liam by the scruff of the neck and giving a shake to make it clear he could easily snap his spine. "Or the shifters. My witch friends fixed me up real good on spells and hex bags to keep people from seeing things that are none of their business. No one's gonna find this place—at least, not until we're long gone."

Liam's hopes sank. He'd wondered how the Huntsman could elude both shifters and psychics, but he didn't know how to counter witchcraft. Then again, if the man's business lay in trapping and trafficking supernatural creatures, it shouldn't have been a surprise that he would have unusual resources at his disposal.

"You got away from me in Ithaca. That made the hunt more interesting." The man stalked through the forest like he owned it, taking Liam farther into the woods. About a quarter mile from where Liam and the male fox had stopped, a ramshackle cabin squatted among the trees. It looked like it might have been a hiker way station back in the day, long abandoned. Two fresh fox pelts hung from stretching racks by the door. The motorcycle Liam had spotted at the lake house fire was parked next to the cabin.

"You're worth the effort," the man continued as he opened the door. Liam's night vision gave him an advantage, but what he saw made his fear spike.

Several large, sturdy cages lined the walls. In one, a large, very furry white and black cat lay dejectedly, barely sparing them a glance as they entered. In another, a muscular spotted wild cat paced, lowering its head to glare at its captor.

The man pushed Liam into one of the empty cages. The wires looked far too thick to chew through, and much too close to slip between.

"You know why? Because I get paid twice for you. Your ex-boyfriend is paying me to kill you. I mighta outsourced that a little. There's a trophy hunter who specializes in 'exotics' who loves hunting fox shifters on his ranch in Montana. He's paying for you to be delivered alive, and then he'll take care of the killing part. I walk away with a nice bonus."

Liam tried to hiss and found it hard to manage even a croak.

"The tranquilizer will wear off eventually. The cages have witchy sigils marked on the metal to keep you from shifting. Now that I've got you, I can pack up my operation and get the hell out of this jerkwater town."

He leered at Liam. "Although, I think I'll be back. Too many shifters here, and trophy hunters go for all kinds. Like that wolf I saw you with. Oh, yeah, I've been keeping tabs. Part of the game. I have some customers who'd love a good hunt for one of those."

"I've had my eye on a couple of places to torch next," the Huntsman went on. "They'll be so busy with the fires, no one will notice my ATV hauling the cages down to the old road, or pay attention when I drive out of town. It's not hard to park a truck with a hauler there, and once I've loaded up the bike, ATV, and cages, no one will be the wiser. I'll take you out of here on a plane from a private airstrip, and collect my fee."

He sighed as if already imagining how he would spend the money.

"I've been in this business for a long time. Never been hired to make a hit before. But you know, I kinda like it. Branching out is good for business," he added, laughing at his own joke.

Liam tried to steady his breathing, which was about the only thing he could control. His body remained paralyzed, and he couldn't even manage to twitch his whiskers. But fortunately, the tracker was still in his mouth, and he hoped with all his heart that it was saliva-resistant.

I've got to do something. If he gets us on that plane, we're dead. If he puts our cages on his ATV, we're as good as dead. Russ is laid up, and it might take a while for Jeffries to convince anyone to listen—or for them to get here. I've got to figure out a way for us to save ourselves.

But at the moment, drugged and frightened, Liam had no clue how to make that happen.

8

RUSS

"HOLD UP A MINUTE! WHAT DO YOU MEAN THE FIRES AND THE MISSING hikers might be connected? And why would a Huntsman be after Liam?" Sheriff Torben Armel held up a hand, and everyone in the room fell silent.

It didn't take a lot of imagination to see Armel as a brown bear. His tall, solid frame, broad shoulders, powerful arms, and strong chest certainly brought that image to mind, not to mention a thick head of brown hair. His end-of-day stubble rivaled the beard it took a lot of men a week to grow, and Russ suspected Armel had to shave his neck if the pelt of dark chest hair at the collar of his shirt was any indication of the rest of him.

Russ wished to hell his throat was better. Even with shifter healing and medication, he still felt groggy, and it hurt to talk. Drew gave him a pitying look, but Russ knew he didn't have a choice.

Liam was in danger.

"He told me—" Russ started, his voice a painful rasp.

Rich Jeffries put up a hand. "Why don't you let me tell the main part, and you can fill in any details I miss?" he asked, trying to save Russ's damaged throat. Russ nodded and made a circular motion with his hand as if to say "get on with it."

Fire Chief Saunders, Sheriff Armel, Russ, and Drew listened as Jeffries recounted Liam's story about the Huntsman his ex had hired, his dramatic escape in Ithaca, and his worry that the hired killer had followed him to Fox Hollow. He added Liam's concern that the missing hikers and the recent spate of arsons were all connected, which drew deep frowns from both officials.

Russ only had to jump in at a few places, but Jeffries's recount matched what Liam had told Russ, with only a few more personal details missing.

"And none of you thought to tell us this, why?" Armel nearly bellowed.

"No proof," Russ growled, finding that pitching his voice lower helped. "It sounds crazy."

"You're right about that," Chief Saunders snapped. Russ had a feeling that if he wasn't already laid out in a hospital bed, injured in the line of duty, Saunders would have ripped him a new one on general principles.

"Is it possible?" Drew asked, looking from the chief to the sheriff. "Just because it sounds far-fetched doesn't make it wrong."

Armel had his arms folded across his chest, but his fingers drummed against his biceps, which Russ had learned was a clear tell that the other man was thinking hard. "I've heard about vengeful exes that tried to arrange to have their former partners killed," he replied. "Takes a certain kind of psycho, but there are all types in the world. So that's possible…although not something you see every day."

"We've never had this many accidental fires in one season," Saunders added, "and never arson. Whoever is setting these fires isn't an amateur. Especially this last one. So the distraction angle is plausible."

"Don't forget—the two hikers are also shifters, and they're both rare types of animals," Jeffries pointed out.

Armel ran a hand back through his thick hair. "Shit. I don't know. Maybe?" He leveled a glare at Jeffries. "And why can't the psychics pick up anything on either the fires or the missing people?"

Jeffries looked like he was considering his words carefully. "There are ways for someone with a knowledge of the occult to hide themselves," he said. "Spells, charms, hex bags—that sort of thing. If this is a Huntsman, I would expect a supernatural bounty hunter to be aware of those tricks, or have allies who could help."

"I thought Huntsmen were just the boogeymen parents used to frighten children that didn't behave." Saunders threw his hands up into the air in frustration, and then turned and began to pace the small hospital room.

"I've done some research since Liam came to me with his story," Jeffries replied. "While a legend has grown up around Huntsmen that probably exaggerates some details, I have found reason to believe that the legend is based on fact. Meaning—it's possible that they're real."

"Fuck," Armel muttered under his breath.

Jeffries's phone pinged. He glanced down and dismissed the new text, then froze and his eyes widened. "Guys, we've got trouble."

"What?" Drew asked.

Russ felt a chill run down his spine, sure something bad had happened to Liam.

"I can't believe I missed this," Jeffries fretted. "I was working, and I didn't pay attention to my phone—"

"What?" this time, Saunders and Armel asked in unison, voices rising in a commanding tone.

"Liam sent this two hours ago. He says he was going to go look for wild foxes to see if they had seen anything to help find the missing hikers."

"Shit," Russ growled.

"He gave me the coordinates and the log-in for his phone GPS, and he said he intended to take a tracker with him somehow when he shifted."

"Like that key-finder you told me about," Drew said with a groan. "Except I don't know how he'd keep one on him as a fox."

"Let's just hope he managed," Armel replied. He looked at Jeffries. "Call him."

Jeffries obliged, setting the phone on speaker. They all heard the repeated ringing, and then Liam's cheery voice, "This is Liam Reynard. Please leave a message."

"Goddammit!" Armel roared. "When will civilians learn that they aren't the fucking Hardy Boys?"

Russ used one hand to hit the call button by his bed, while he leaned on the other hand to help him sit up. A nurse bustled into the room, looking at him with alarm. "What's going on?"

"I'm signing myself out," Russ answered, swinging his legs out of bed.

"The doctor needs to approve—"

"Then sign me out AMA," Russ growled. He looked to Drew. "Find me some pants, or you all get to see my full moon." The nurse fixed him with a disapproving look and hurried out as Drew ransacked the drawers of the nightstand and came up with a pair of scrubs.

"Where do you think you're going?" Chief Saunders demanded.

"With you, to find Liam and kick the Huntsman's ass."

Drew stayed close as Russ maneuvered so he could pull on the pants without giving everyone a free show. Russ felt proud that although he still felt like he'd been hit by a truck, he didn't need help to get dressed.

"What's all this?" A harried-looking doctor came into the room just a few steps behind the same nurse they had seen minutes before. "Why are you out of bed?"

Russ turned to the doctor. "Am I in any danger?"

The doctor looked taken aback. "No, but—"

"Then I'm signing myself out."

"You've healed quickly, as I'd expect from a shifter, but I would advise remaining under observation for another night—"

"I can walk. I can breathe. I can even almost talk," Russ grated. "So give me my papers."

"I need to note that this is against medical advice," the physician huffed.

"Noted. Now someone find me my damn shoes."

The two medical professionals exchanged a look, and the doctor shrugged. The nurse came over and removed the IV from Russ's hand. "I was afraid you'd do something like this. So I've already got pharmacy bringing up your medications. Don't try to leave without them, or I'll put you back on your ass so fast you won't know what hit you," she added without looking up, making it clear that his wolf didn't intimidate her in the slightest.

That's what you get for having a badger shifter for a nurse.

Chief Saunders turned to glower at Russ. "How do you think you're going to manage? You look like you can barely stay on your feet."

"Liam's my true mate," Russ replied, meeting the chief's gaze. "I don't care if I have to crawl. I'm going to rescue him."

"Seriously?" Armel rumbled. "Because I am not going to carry you out if you fall flat on your face. Is that clear?"

"Crystal," Russ snapped. Armel was a good guy and a fair sheriff, but his bear shifter side tended to try to roll right over people when he got his dander up.

Russ realized Jeffries had been texting. "You hear something from Liam?"

Jeffries shook his head. "No. I activated the tracker app Liam sent me. It should work—as long as we're close enough."

Russ gave him a skeptical look, sure he had seen the professor typing, but let it go. "Come on. We've got people to save."

He managed to make it out of his room without help, gathering his will and stubbornly refusing to give in to the remaining soreness. When they walked out of the hospital's front doors, Russ was not prepared for the sight that awaited them.

At least fifteen people—all shifters—had turned out, dressed for a hike and armed with shotguns, rifles, and handguns. Weapons weren't unusual in the forest since wild animal attacks did occur from time to time, but Russ wasn't used to seeing his neighbors packing heat.

"What's all this?" Sheriff Armel's voice boomed.

"We're here to find Liam and those hikers," Sherri answered, giving her cousin a defiant look that dared him to argue. "We all are."

Everyone in the crowd nodded. "We want to save Liam," Maddi added, and Linda nodded. Russ looked around and saw Brandon and Ty, as well as some of the other guys from the firehouse. Even Woody from the diner stood with the others, looking pale, scared, and resolute.

"This isn't a lark," the sheriff warned. "We believe the person who may have taken Liam and the hikers is a professional criminal. He's armed and very dangerous."

"We don't have to engage," Sherri countered. "We can surround, harry, and track. Linda's the best damn tracking dog in the county."

Linda nodded. "My nose is as good as ever, even if the muzzle is a little gray." Russ thought he recalled that the library volunteer was a beagle shifter.

Armel looked to Saunders, as if for support. The fire chief shrugged. "Wouldn't be the first time someone deputized a posse to hunt down a poacher."

Sheriff Armel growled deep in his throat, but he seemed to know a lost cause when he saw it. Russ figured that if they didn't organize the crowd, their neighbors would just follow on their own.

"All right," the sheriff grumbled. "You can come along. But listen up. We'll go in the department's SUVs, and you can leave your clothing and weapons in the vehicles. Shift when we get there. We have coordinates of the place where Liam planned to go. He might have a GPS tracker on him, but it's got limited range, so noses to the ground will be more help at the beginning."

"If this is the same person who's been burning things down, can we bite—a little—if we bring him down?" Ty asked, with a feral smile that reminded Russ of his friend's inner bobcat.

"Only as necessary to subdue the suspect," Armel warned. A disappointed murmur spread through the crowd. They were ready for blood to punish someone who had hurt one of their own, and Russ realized that was just another reason he loved this town.

Russ and Drew got into one of the SUVs at the police station, along with Linda, Maddi, Woody, and a few other folks Russ knew from town. Ty's mom was at the hospital with Justin, but Ty's dad had turned out, as had the Thompson brothers from The Lone Coyote.

"You don't look so good," Drew said under his breath.

"I'll be a lot better when we have Liam back safe and sound."

Jeffries rode in the front SUV with Armel, although he had shared the tracker app with someone in each group. Since the psychic couldn't shift, he had offered to stay with the cars and coordinate the clairvoyants from the Institute who had volunteered to turn their focus on the missing men. The three SUVs formed a convoy, heading to the parking lot of the trailhead where the hikers went missing.

No one spoke on the ride. Russ's worries about Liam consumed his thoughts, and he guessed that Drew was equally concerned about the way he had checked himself out AMA. Russ knew he wasn't at a hundred percent, even though his shifter metabolism was working hard to heal. But Liam was missing, as were two other men. Russ had pushed himself beyond his limits before, for less.

If their guess was right and this was a Huntsman, then bringing him to justice wouldn't just avenge the injury done to Liam and the hikers, but it would stop a much larger web of crimes against shifters.

Russ had heard the Huntsman legends—he figured all shifter children grew up with them, dire warnings to keep their other self a secret, to stay close to their territory, to be wary of those who weren't also supernatural creatures. *Be careful, or the Huntsman will carry you off.*

Those old tales, viewed through the lens of adulthood, revealed a much more terrifying reality, Russ realized. *Not just someone who hunted shifters for sport—bad enough. Someone who procures shifters for rich hunters. Shifter trafficking.*

And right now, Liam was at that man's mercy. Everything in Russ's nature strained against that knowledge. He wanted to shift, and biting wasn't the worst of what he wanted to do to the Huntsman.

He has our mate. Russ wanted to rip the Huntsman limb from limb, tear out his throat, shred his body with sharp claws. Make an example of him so no one ever forgot what happened to someone who tried to come between fated mates.

"Easy," Drew murmured, laying a hand on Russ's shoulder, steadying him with the reassurance of pack.

Russ felt a rush of shame that he had focused only on what the Huntsman had done to Liam. Justin was Russ's misfit pack as well, and the Huntsman had tried to kill him—kill both of them—with the set fires and the weakened beams. Russ wanted vengeance for Justin as well.

"Looks like we're here," Rusty Thompson said as he pulled in to park beside the sheriff's SUV in the trailhead lot, and Liam's Honda Civic. They spilled out of the vehicles and shifted right away. No one stared, and no one felt ashamed. Shifters were less concerned with modesty than outsiders, perhaps because their animal selves had no understanding of the concept.

Shifting hurt Russ more than usual, given the damage the fire had done to his body, but once he was in his wolf form, his injuries faded quickly. *Shifting is the best medicine.* While his human body was usually strong and healthy, wearing his wolf gave Russ an extra sense of confidence and an innate skill that took all of his abilities to a completely different level.

Despite the seriousness of the situation, Russ felt the excitement in the group. All of the shifters who had turned out were predators of one kind or another, from bear to bobcat to Maddi's freaking adorable Main Coon cat. They each had talents to bring to the hunt, and now that the time had come, they were ready to go.

Armel hadn't shifted yet. "Look for Liam's scent. If you find it, bark, yip, howl—do what you do." He slowed and turned to see three foxes standing on the trail. The male stepped forward and then let out a series of barks and whines, agitated and clearly trying his best to communicate.

Russ knew one thing for certain—those foxes weren't shifters.

"I think we've got a break in the case," Armel said to the group. "Everyone, follow the foxes."

They all headed up the trail, following their unexpected guides. Russ shouldered his way to the front, intent on getting to Liam as quickly as he could. Armel came barreling up from behind since he had shifted last, but despite his bulk, the sheriff reminded everyone just how fast a bear could run.

Russ caught a faint whiff of Liam's scent, and he raised his snout to the wind, counting on his sharp wolf senses to help him find his mate. More than that, Russ tried to calm himself enough to test what he had always heard about fated mates—that they possessed a bond which enabled them to come back to one another.

Our connection is new. Is it strong enough? We haven't completed the mating bites. Does that matter?

Russ couldn't let doubt weaken him. He believed Liam would do everything in his power to fight and get free. Russ had to return that faith and prove he was worthy of Liam's love and their mate bond.

If his wolf ever had an opportunity to prove himself, it was now.

9

LIAM

FEELING CAME BACK GRADUALLY, AND WITH IT, MOVEMENT. LIAM HADN'T lost consciousness, so he didn't have to fight through disorientation.

He already knew he was fucked.

After the Huntsman captured him and gloated about his success, he'd chucked Liam into a cage that was big enough for his fox, but far too small to allow him to shift, even without the witch marks that kept him from trying. Now that he had his wits about him, Liam could see that the same was true for the ocelot and lynx, who were also trapped in their cat forms.

Liam didn't have military or law enforcement training, but he had read a lot of books about characters who did, written by writers with personal experience. All that, plus his cozy mystery obsession, gave him a number of alternatives to consider.

On the plus side, he wasn't injured, and the tranquilizer seemed to be wearing off quickly. He was more valuable alive than dead, and his captor was currently gone. Liam thanked his stars that he had sent that message to Jeffries, although as time wore on, he wondered what was taking so long. He had the tracking Tile in his mouth, assuming it still functioned.

Now for the bad news. Being trapped in fox form meant less

manual dexterity and put him at an even greater disadvantage for height and weight against his captor than he'd have had as his human self. He had no weapons. Worst of all, the Huntsman intended to make as quick a getaway as possible and had already gone to get his truck. Time was running out.

Liam heard a ping of metal against metal. He looked down into the tray beneath the wire bottom of the cage to see the spent dart that had brought him down. He stared at it for a moment, and an idea formed.

Using one claw, Liam carefully fished the dart up to where he could reach the butt end of it with his teeth and shifted the small square tracker in his mouth to ride between his cheek and molars. He had been examining the inside of the latch while he lay unable to move and figured out how the locking mechanism worked. His claws were too short to maneuver the latch into position, where it would release the back of the live trap cage. Someone looking to relocate a problem animal without hurting it could throw the latch, roll the cage, and the bottom would open, allowing the animal to escape without close contact with its captor.

The steel dart combined with the strength of Liam's jaws just might be enough to make it work. He maneuvered himself into position and began scraping at the latch, moving it little by little, when his human finger could have pushed it clear in one go.

The process took far too long, considering that their captor could come back at any moment. But Liam feared that if he rushed, he might break the dart or drop it and lose his only chance. He kept at it, although it made his teeth hurt and his jaw ache. His neck spasmed from the odd angle, and one of his whiskers caught in the wire and pulled out, making his muzzle throb.

He had no idea how long he had been working at the lock, although every minute that passed was one closer to when the Huntsman would return. Finally, he felt the latch shift completely and heard the click of the release.

Now to put his victory to the test.

Liam hurled himself as hard as he could against the side of the cage, rocking it on the table. He threw his weight against the wires again and again, until he succeeded in rolling the cage over.

The metal panel sprung open on the bottom, and Liam bolted through, dropping the dart and shaking out his fur in triumph. The tracker remained safe in the pouch of his cheek.

There was no time for a victory dance. Liam needed to shift and open the cages of the other captives so they could run for their lives. He concentrated, picturing his human form, gathering the intention to change as he had always done.

Nothing happened.

He tried again and failed.

Liam's heart pounded, and he felt a flash of panic. Had the Huntsman put him under a spell? Perhaps he had used magic to keep them from shifting inside the cabin? Was the tranquilizer still not completely out of his system? Would whatever locked him in this form be permanent?

With a muted growl, Liam pushed his fear aside and trotted up to the lynx's cage. The large cat lifted its head, watching him closely, then let out a pitiful mew.

Liam studied the lock, but even with his dart, he knew he wouldn't be able to move the bigger, heavier latch. In human form, it wouldn't have required a second thought.

If I can get out of here and get help, opening the cage won't be a problem. Even if I'm stuck in my fur forever.

Much as Liam loved his fox, he loved his human side too. Being human meant books and hamburgers, libraries and ice cream cones, and most of all—Russ.

The tranquilizer left Liam's thoughts fuzzy, and he wondered if that kept Russ from sensing his fear and danger through their link. He had read somewhere that true mates had a psychic and emotional bond that grew stronger over time, and could be almost telepathic. Liam remembered wishing he might find something like that for himself one day, and then losing hope that such a connection could exist.

Magic. The Huntsman said he used magic to keep the psychics from finding him. Maybe that same magic blocks my bond to Russ—if we even have one, with everything being so new. Would it be stronger if we would have completed our mating? If I'd bitten him?

Liam knew he needed to get out of there. With a whimper and a whine—his best shot at assuring the two cats he would come back for them—Liam made for the door.

He feared another lock to defeat, but the choice of a ramshackle shed meant the structure was practically falling down on itself. The old wood had warped, leaving a small gap. It didn't look big enough, but Liam knew he could wriggle through.

With a burst of adrenaline, Liam ran for the hole—just as the door opened and the Huntsman filled the doorway.

"Fuck! What are you doing out?"

Liam changed course, trying to dodge around the man's legs and make a break for freedom. His captor slammed the door shut and grabbed for Liam, but Liam twisted, evading the grasping hands, trying to go for the hole at the bottom. The man's boot moved to block the way, and Liam barely missed getting stepped on.

"Come back here, you little shit!"

Strategy fled as self-preservation took over. Liam jumped on top of the big cats' cages, and from there to a shelf on the wall. The rusted nails holding the ledge gave way, and Liam flailed as he fell, then managed to land on a table. His paws hit loose papers, and he slid, sending a pack of shotgun shells flying off the edge and spilling the cartridges across the floor.

"I'm gonna skin you alive!"

The Huntsman moved fast, but Liam ran faster, leaping from the desk to the top of an old wooden dresser, and then onto another shelf. He held his breath as the old wood creaked with the force of his landing, and he eyed his next move.

He saw the Huntsman reaching for a weapon. Liam didn't know whether the man was going for a shotgun or his tranquilizer rifle, and he didn't want to find out. He leaped for the curtain rod above the window, then dug his claws into the filthy cloth to control his fall, shredding the flimsy old cotton with his weight.

As soon as his paws touched the ground, Liam was off and running, this time staying beneath the cabin's furnishings and weaving around stacks of empty cages and boxes of supplies. The Huntsman veered after him, and Liam bumped into the pile of cages, rebounding quickly. The jolt was enough to make the stack wobble and send the top cage crashing down, clipping the Huntsman on his shoulder.

"That's it! I don't give a fuck about the second bounty. Gonna kill you like I was hired to do. You hear me?"

Liam heard. He had managed to lead his captor on a chase around the small cabin, moving stealthily beneath the bed and desk to evade notice. Now he was closer to the door than the Huntsman, and Liam took his chance.

He bolted for the door and dove for the hole at full speed, belly-crawling to make it through to freedom. Just as he began to push his hindquarters through the gap, the Huntsman grabbed his tail and yanked him back. The rough wood scraped against Liam's fur, and the grip on his tail wrenched his spine, but he doubled forward, in the most amazing ab crunch he had ever managed, and sank his teeth into the fleshy side of the Huntsman's hand.

"Fucker!"

The Huntsman relaxed his grip for just a second, allowing Liam to slide through. He hit the ground and ran behind the most solid thing in the room, the old desk.

"I am through with this bullshit." The Huntsman racked a shell into a shotgun. Liam had no illusions about how much damage that would do. The kidnapper shot once, blasting away part of the panel in the back of the kneehole. Luckily, Liam was crouched behind the drawers, but they would only hold the hunter off for so long.

He shot again, deafeningly close. The buckshot sent up a hail of splinters as it tore into the drawers.

Liam had nowhere to run. Nothing else in the room was heavy enough to keep the Huntsman from just tossing it out of the way. In a few more shots, the desk would be damaged enough that it would either fall apart or would be easy to move. He could try dodging around the room again, but that would cost him far more energy than it required from his adversary, who only had to wait for Liam to tire.

Liam cowered behind the desk, knowing that time had run out. One more shot, maybe two, and it would be over. Kelson had finally won, but his revenge bit deeper than just taking Liam's life. Dying now meant never seeing Russ again, never exploring their connection, or discovering what it truly meant to be fated mates.

Liam didn't want to leave Russ, and he wondered how his lover would cope with losing Liam after he had already buried Anthony. Liam strained to sense anything from Russ through their bond, but whether it was the newness of the connection or some dark magic of the Huntsman's, he remained utterly alone.

The Huntsman racked his gun once more. Liam braced for the end.

I love you, Russ. I'm so sorry we didn't get to be together. Remember me.

10

RUSS

RUSS KEPT PACE WITH THE BEAR AND THE BEAGLE, FOLLOWING THE MALE fox on a race up the trail and then off into the forest. He heard the others not far behind, and pitied the three deputies who brought up the rear, still in human form so they could handle phones and weapons.

The beagle kept her nose to the ground, clearly following Liam's scent. Far behind them, the deputies had the tracking app open, so if Liam's hare-brained idea of taking a key-finder with him actually worked, they would be able to pick up on it once they got within range. Armel wore an earpiece specially designed for shifters so his deputies could communicate with him, in case the tracker got a fix on Liam's position.

Russ concentrated on his connection to Liam. He was certain that after they made love, he had caught glimpses of Liam's feelings, along with an uncanny sense of his lover's proximity and mood. If they'd both been merely human, Russ might have shrugged it off as the intensity of new love. But being shifters changed everything. He'd heard stories about fated mates like he'd heard the legend of the Huntsman, paying scant attention to either. Now it seemed fate intended to prove that some legends were real.

Suddenly, the fox stopped and swung its head to indicate they should continue. Whatever lay before them scared their guide too much for him to go on.

Russ whined, lowering his head in a bow of thanks. He wondered if foxes were close enough to canines to have the same "root language" of gestures. The fox nodded, then padded off and disappeared into the forest.

Russ stood close enough to the sheriff to hear the message through his earpiece.

"We've got a lock on the tracker. One hundred feet, straight ahead."

Liam and I haven't even run together in our fur. Haven't seen each other's animals up close. Haven't done so much. Please, anyone up there who's listening, bring him back to me.

The beagle made it clear that she had picked up the trail. Russ and Armel started running again, pulling farther ahead of the others.

A shotgun blast echoed through the forest, frightening a flock of birds from the trees.

Russ and the sheriff exchanged a look and picked up speed. Russ wanted to howl his rage, but he choked back the sound in case they still had a chance of surprising the Huntsman.

Another blast sounded. Russ felt his heart in his throat. If the Huntsman was still shooting, that meant Liam must still be alive, but he worried Liam's luck would run out soon.

Just as they came within the last few feet of a tumbledown cabin, a third shot rang out.

Sheriff Armel barreled into the door at full bear speed, taking it right off its hinges. Russ leaped through the opening seconds later, head down, teeth bared, hackles raised, ready to fight.

Russ glimpsed a tall, muscular man with a shotgun swinging his weapon in their direction to fire at point-blank range. Before the man could pull the trigger, a red cloud of hissing fury appeared in a streak from somewhere, wrapping itself around the man's face and head as it bit and scratched like something possessed.

Armel hurtled forward, hitting the man center mass and knocking him to the floor. Russ lunged for the hand that held the shotgun, staying away from the muzzle of the weapon as he chomped down hard on their attacker's wrist, crunching bone and sinew with his powerful jaws and sharp teeth.

The little red rage demon wrapped around their attacker's head continued to hiss, yip, claw, and bite, and the Huntsman bucked and fought, trying to throw off Russ and Liam until Armel settled the matter by sitting on his hips.

With a brown bear pinning his lower body, his right wrist a bloody ruin from Russ's bite, and his face and scalp shredded from Liam's manic attack, the Huntsman finally went slack beneath the combined assault, signaling surrender.

Russ didn't like leaving anything to chance. He stepped to one side and shifted, then picked up the shotgun and checked to make sure it had a shell chambered.

"Move, and I shoot," he growled. "Liam...it's okay. We're here. You can stop mauling him now."

The fox slowly uncurled from around the Huntsman's head. Russ let out a low whistle when he got a look at the damage. Deep bites left parts of the man's scalp hanging loose, while long gashes ran down both sides of his face, and an ear had a bloody notch out of it.

Liam ducked back under the desk for a second, then padded up to Russ, still in his fox form, and sat at his feet, looking up at him with a mix of fear and desperation in his amber eyes. Blood matted Liam's fur, and Russ couldn't tell whether any of it belonged to Liam or if it was all from the Huntsman. Liam opened his mouth, and Russ thought he might be sick, but then a small black square landed on the floor—the tracker that helped to lead them here. Russ figured Liam had stashed it beneath the desk when he attacked the Huntsman and went back to retrieve it just now.

Outside, a chorus of barks, howls, yips, and screeches celebrated their victory. Three human deputies crowded into the room, weapons drawn, to find a bear pinning their quarry to the ground, a blood-stained fox, and a naked man holding a shotgun pointed at the Huntsman.

"You can lower your gun now, Russ," Carter Franks, Armel's deputy, said. "Both of them," he added with a smirk and a glance that reminded Russ he wasn't wearing any clothing.

The bear glowered at Carter, who immediately sobered. "Sorry, Sheriff."

Russ snatched a faded blanket from the cot and wrapped it around his waist. He set the shotgun on the desk, then he knelt down to be as close as possible to eye-level with Liam.

"Are you alright?" he asked. Behind him, he heard Armel shuffle off, freeing their prisoner so the deputies could cuff the Huntsman and pat him down.

Liam managed a curt nod, but Russ saw how his body trembled. "I promise, I'll get you out of here just as soon as I can," Russ told him.

"Guess we found the missing hikers," Carter said, drawing Russ's attention to the other side of the cabin. He saw the lynx and the ocelot in their cages, where both had huddled as far away from the fight as possible.

Drew, still in his wolf form, and Ty, still a bobcat, milled around at the front of the crowd, clearly anxious to see that Russ and Liam were unharmed.

Carter hunkered down in front of the big cats' cages. "We're the good guys. We're here to rescue you. I'd like to take you back to town and have a doctor look you over. So when I let you out, remember that, and don't try to eat me, okay?"

He opened the cage doors, and the two kidnapped hikers slowly sauntered out. They looked tense until they got a good view of the Huntsman, bloodied and restrained, clearly in custody. Then both creatures began to purr, a deep rumbling sound that filled the cabin.

"Jackson," Carter said, indicating one of the other deputies. "Take Russ, Drew, Liam, and Ty down to one of the SUVs along with the two hikers. Drew and Ty—you're the hikers' new buddies while we get this sorted out. Let's get them to the hospital and have the docs check them over. There should be a couple of sets of one-size-fits-all emergency clothing in the duffel in the cargo area. Then come back and tag-team with Emery to get all the folks back to town," he said to the deputies, with a nod toward their friends and neighbors. "I'll finish up here with the sheriff and take care of the prisoner."

Russ noticed that Carter had a light backpack which probably included clothing for the sheriff. Shifters might be less prudish than regular humans, but that didn't mean anyone wanted to see their sheriff handling police business in the buff.

Russ reached toward Liam, and the fox nuzzled his open palm. Something was still wrong, but Russ wasn't sure what it could be. The fear hadn't left Liam's eyes, which worried Russ. *What does he know that we don't?*

"Come on," Jackson said, and his designated passengers all trooped out after him. Russ shifted back to his wolf, and kept pace with Liam, staying close. Deputy Emery followed with the next group of towns-folk behind him.

At the moment, Liam looked worse for the wear, with his fur matted with blood and covered with a layer of dirt as if he had shim-mied beneath the furnishings. *And maybe he did, trying not to get shot.* Russ couldn't see any open wounds, but Liam carried himself stiffly as if his hips were sore, and his tail stayed down, almost limp.

Russ whined softly, worried about Liam. The fox looked at him and yipped, intentionally bumping into his shoulder. *Once we're fully mated, we won't have to worry about a vulpine-to-lupine translation guide,* he thought. *Charades is a lot harder to play without hands.*

When they reached the parking lot, everyone else peeled off to find their clothing and shift back to human. Jeffries jumped out of the SUV where he'd been waiting and hurried over to Liam as Russ went to retrieve his things and get dressed. Russ could still hear the harried professor as he fussed over Liam.

"Liam? Oh my God, is that blood? Are you injured?" Jeffries asked. "You were right, weren't you? About all of it. I'm sorry I took so long. I wasn't expecting your text, and I didn't look at my phone right away. As soon as I saw it, I called in reinforcements."

Russ laid a hand on Jeffries's shoulder. "You did good, Rich. We wouldn't have known what was going on if you hadn't relayed the text. You saved their lives."

Jeffries watched the lynx and the ocelot slink over to the SUV, where Jackson dug baggy T-shirts and elastic-waist basketball shorts out of an emergency duffel. Russ went to retrieve a set for Liam and held them out. "C'mon. Go behind the truck and shift. Got clothes for you."

Liam whined, and Russ frowned, trying to decipher the noise. "You're afraid to shift?" He guessed. Liam shook his head. "You don't think you can shift?" A nod. Russ felt fear thrum through him. He'd heard legends about shifters getting locked in one form or another. If the Huntsman legend had been real, could the other be true, too?

If so, then I've got a pet fox instead of a life partner. I am not going to accept that without a fight.

Jeffries knelt in front of Liam. "The psychics believe that the man who took you was using some kind of spells or occult sigils to hide you from us. If he had that type of knowledge, it's possible he had wardings that also kept you from being able to shift. Will you try again now? Please?"

Russ felt his heart in his throat as Liam shook himself from snout to tail, and noticed again how he favored his hips. Then the fox closed his eyes, and Russ held his breath. The lynx and the ocelot moved closer, watching as if they shared Liam's fear.

He had never seen his mate shift before, so Russ had no way to know whether anything was amiss. The process seemed slower than what he thought of as normal, but he didn't know if it varied from Liam's norm. Then it was over, and a very human Liam lay naked and streaked with blood, curled on his side on the pavement.

"Liam!" Russ rushed forward, trying to make sure Liam was all right and also shield him from onlookers.

"He kept us from shifting," Liam said through tears, as his shoulders shook. Russ gathered him into his arms and held him tight, rocking him like a child. "And then I picked the lock, but I couldn't free the others, and I tried to get away, but he yanked so hard on my tail…and he said he was going to skin me."

Russ's anger burned hot, rising even beyond his rage when he and Drew were disowned by the pack. He was glad he hadn't stayed behind with the sheriff. The temptation to mete out his own punishment might have been beyond his ability to resist.

Mate. Protect. His wolf paced in his mind, clearly in favor of rougher justice.

"Shh," Russ soothed, stroking Liam's hair, heedless of the blood that matted it in places. He wrapped his arm around Liam and pulled him tight. "Let's get you dressed, and take you to the hospital. Make sure you're okay. And then I'm taking you home with me." *For good*, he added silently, even though he wasn't sure Liam was quite ready for that step.

Liam clung to him, burying his face in Russ's chest, heaving with quiet sobs. Gradually, he stilled.

"You ready?" Russ asked quietly. Liam nodded. Russ steadied him as he pulled on a top and shorts, noting how he winced from bending or twisting. He remembered how Liam's luxurious tail had hung down behind him and prayed that the damage wasn't permanent.

Russ pulled Liam against him, hugging tight. Liam slipped his arms around him and squeezed back. "You scared the shit out of me," Russ murmured. "And then I heard him shooting, and I was afraid we were too late. I thought I lost you," he added, letting one hand rub soothing circles down Liam's back.

"I didn't think I'd make it out of there," Liam whispered. "And all I could think about was wanting to come home to you, not wanting to leave you."

"It's over," Russ soothed. "And we're together. The sooner we get you to the hospital and feeling better, the sooner we can go home, together."

Russ helped Liam into the SUV. He felt relieved when the ocelot and lynx were also able to shift; a handsome, slender Latinx man and another man with long blond hair appeared. Ty and Drew stuck close to them, taking their roles as protectors seriously.

Liam said nothing on the ride to the hospital, resting his head on Russ's shoulder. Russ just stroked one hand up and down Liam's arm, pressing his face into Liam's hair, grateful to have his mate back, safe and alive.

"I'm sorry," Liam murmured, barely loud enough for Russ to hear. "I shouldn't have gone alone. I just wanted to find out where he was and then leave, but he tranqued me. The next thing I knew, he was shaking me and telling me all the things he was going to do to me."

Russ knew he stiffened in anger and that Liam felt it. He closed his eyes, breathing deeply, trying to rein in his fury.

"It's not your fault," Russ replied. "He was going to come for you no matter where you were. But you told Jeffries where you were going. Why didn't you text me?" He couldn't keep the hurt out of his voice, although he suspected that he already knew the reason.

"You were in the hospital, healing. I didn't want to worry you. It was supposed to be a quick run, in and out. Then I was going to tell you all about it, and figure out what to do from there."

"Not your fault," Russ repeated. "You still found the Huntsman, led us to him, and kept him from killing anyone or spiriting them away until we got there. And then, holy fuck, you were badass. My little red demon. I thought you were going to chew off his nose."

Liam managed a sniffly chuckle. "I would have. He was going to shoot you. I couldn't let him do that."

Russ tightened his hold on his mate. Scared, hurt, and weaponless, Liam had still risked everything to save him, and his daring attack had kept him and the sheriff from being shot, possibly killed. "So proud of you," he whispered.

"Bite me," Liam replied.

"What?" Russ started to pull back. Liam hung on, not letting go.

"I want your mating bite. I know it hasn't been long, and if you're not ready, I understand, but when you are, I'm yours," Liam whispered. "That was my biggest regret when I thought I'd never see you again. That I had held back, and maybe we would never have the chance."

Russ shook his head. "Baby, you've got nothing to apologize for. There's no timetable. When you're ready, I'm ready. I'm not going anywhere without you."

Liam settled against him for the rest of the ride, as if the events of the day had finally caught up to him. He might have even dozed. Russ jostled him gently when they pulled into the hospital parking lot.

"We're here," he said into Liam's ear. "Feels like I just left. Maybe they'll name a room after me," he joked.

Liam clung harder, and Russ ran a soothing hand down his arm. "I'm going to stay with you, come hell or high water, you hear me?" He took Liam's hand and threaded their fingers together.

Russ guessed that one of the deputies had called ahead to let the hospital in Fox Hollow know they were coming. Nurses and orderlies met them at the emergency room door and whisked Liam and the two hikers off for examination. Russ folded himself into a chair to wait, and Drew sat beside him.

"I promised Carlos, the ocelot, that I'd be here when he's done," Ty said, walking up to them with his hands shoved into his pockets. "But I figured since we have to wait, I could go see how Justin is doing."

Russ nodded. "Sounds good. We'll tell Carlos that you'll be back. Let Justin know we're thinking of him."

For the moment, the waiting area was quiet, probably a pause between waves of activity. Drew put a hand on Russ's shoulder. "How are you? And how do you think Liam is?"

Now that the rescue was over, Russ felt himself crashing. He had been well on his way to healing before he checked himself out, and shifting helped take his recovery further, but the trauma of the fire and then Liam's near-death experience left him exhausted. Worry for Liam gnawed at him, and inside his head, his wolf paced, angry he couldn't stay by Liam's side.

He gave a humorless chuckle. "I'm a mess," Russ replied. "Liam and I both nearly got killed. It was too damn close, man. I can't stop my brain from running all the alternate endings—and none of them are good." He leaned forward, resting his elbows on his knees, and let his head hang.

"My wolf is totally freaked out. And maybe it's part of this whole 'fated mates' thing, but I swear I can feel some of Liam's emotions through our growing bond...and he's putting on a brave front, but he's not in a good place."

"Can't blame him for that," Drew replied. "But he's alive. So are you and the two hikers. We caught the Huntsman. And you know this will be a Tribunal case because there's no way the sheriff can send it through the normal channels."

Sheriff Armel still didn't have a name for the Huntsman, or any details, although Russ knew he had his people and the city police working on it. Having the arsons tied together with the shifter-hunting piece was going to play merry hell with how they could file charges, and affect settling insurance claims.

When a crime in the supernatural community could not be prosecuted through human channels without revealing the existence of the paranormal, a tribunal convened in Albany to try the case. The judges were elders, chosen for their knowledge related to the situation, empowered to hand down a binding verdict—up to and including a death sentence.

"I know. And I can't imagine they'll let him off. But what I want to know is, how did Liam's ex get connected to a Huntsman? I mean, you see stories all the time of people who thought they were hiring a regular hitman and end up with an undercover cop instead. There's something fishy. His ex wasn't even a shifter."

Drew frowned. "Yeah, that doesn't smell right. He had to know someone inside the shifter community to even find out about a Huntsman, let alone be able to get in touch with one."

Russ rubbed his temples, wishing it would ease his headache. "Maybe the sheriff will find something that helps him track the Huntsman's connections. I hate to think that Liam's ex might try again." He felt antsy, desperate for an update on Liam's condition, and it took all of Russ's willpower not to pace like his inner wolf.

"So did you get a chance to talk much with the lynx?" Russ needed to change the topic.

Drew nodded. "A little. He's probably worse off than Liam since he got grabbed several days earlier. His name is Noah. He's on vacation from Canada, and he's a wildlife photographer."

"A shifter who takes pictures of other animals?"

Drew shrugged. "No one thinks it's strange when people take pictures of other people."

"You've got a good point."

"I…um…told him he could stay with us for a couple of days while he recovered and got his plans together," Drew admitted. "I know it makes it a little crowded if Liam's with you, but Noah can have my room, and I'll sleep on the couch. It's just, he doesn't know anyone here, and he's a long way from home."

"We'll make it work," Russ promised. Offering was the decent thing to do. Still, it occurred to Russ that it had been a long time since he'd seen his brother do something unexpected. *Did Drew see something he liked?* he wondered. He would pay more attention to the lynx the next time he saw him if this might be someone his brother was interested in. All he glimpsed during the ride to the hospital was a mane of very blond hair and a full beard.

Floofy, his wolf supplied, with the canine equivalent of a snicker.

Oh yeah, if Drew hooks up with a big cat, there will be plenty of jokes. They practically write themselves, Russ thought.

He remembered Drew's earlier comment about having given up on finding someone for himself and having his faith restored because Russ had found Liam. Whether Drew's someone special turned out to be Noah or not, Russ hoped his brother would find his own fated mate.

Russ heard movement and looked up as the doctor left Liam's room. "Dr. Fisher!" he called, jumping out of the chair and jogging up to catch him before he could vanish. "How is he?"

The physician gave him a kind smile but shook his head. "Russ, you know I can't discuss his situation with you, not without the right paperwork. But he's resting now, and you can go see him. We're working up his discharge orders, so giving him a ride home would be a big help."

"Oh, believe me, I was planning on it." Russ let out a long exhale. "Thank you." He headed for Liam's room and paused in the doorway.

Liam still wore the borrowed clothing the deputy had given him, but at least he hadn't needed to change into one of those damn bare-ass hospital gowns. He looked haggard, as if all his energy and his usual fox fabulousness had been drained out of him. That just made Russ want to pound the Huntsman to smithereens even more.

"Hey," Russ called quietly from just inside the room. Liam opened his eyes and managed a tired smile.

"Hey," he replied, holding out his hand.

Having just been in a hospital bed himself only hours before, Russ did a quick assessment to gauge Liam's condition. He felt relieved that there weren't any monitors or IV lines hooked up.

"How're you feeling?" Russ smoothed his thumb over the back of Liam's hand.

"I've been better," Liam said. "But I'd have been a lot worse if you guys hadn't shown up when you did."

Russ nodded, unable to get the words past the lump in his throat.

"They told me to hydrate, take ibuprofen, and get some rest," Liam told him. "The good news is that there's nothing wrong with my tail except some pulled muscles. Doc said that the pills would help with that, and recommended a massage and a hot bath." His lips quirked into a mischievous grin. "Think I might be able to get some help with that?"

Russ leaned down to kiss his forehead. "I think I can manage," he murmured, letting his fingers trail down the side of Liam's face.

Russ heard footsteps and straightened as a nurse—the same badger shifter who had taken care of him—came in pushing an empty wheelchair. She gave Russ a slit-eyed glare as she fussed over Liam.

"I have your prescription and your discharge papers," she told Liam and glanced at Russ skeptically. "Are you here to take him home?"

"Sure am," Russ replied. "Anything I need to know to watch out for?"

"It's all on the discharge papers," she said, handing an envelope to Liam. "You might want to stop off at the pharmacy and get that prescription filled on your way. The dose we gave you will wear off in a few hours, and it works best if you don't let the soreness get ahead of you. Call if you have any questions."

"You ready?" Russ asked when she was gone.

"More than ready to go home."

"Your place or mine?"

"Yours, if it's okay?" Liam asked. "My house is…not as private. I want to be away from everyone for a little bit. Jeffries talked to the committee, and they told me to take the rest of the week off."

"I'd love to bring you home with me," Russ assured him, privately glad Liam chose that option. "Besides, we have a much bigger bathtub." He thanked fate that remodeling the bathroom had been one of the first projects he and Drew completed when they bought the house.

"That sounds really nice."

Liam allowed Russ to steady him to get from the bed to the wheelchair. Russ figured Liam had every right to be a little shaky after what he'd been through and was grateful that he didn't put up a fuss. He parked Liam's wheelchair at the curb and went to retrieve his vehicle to pick him up.

"Drew brought the truck over," he answered Liam's unspoken question when he pulled up beside him. Russ eyed the high step to get into the cab. "You need a hand? Drew and I can go back and fetch your car once we get you settled."

"I can manage," Liam replied. "I think. And my car keys are in the pocket of the jeans I rolled up and stashed behind the restroom at the trailhead parking lot. You'll need them."

"We'll get your clothes, the keys, and the car," Russ assured him.

Russ hovered behind him, just in case, but Liam got himself into the truck, although Russ suspected it might have been sheer willpower. Liam dozed as they waited at the drive-thru pharmacy for his prescription, and Russ watched him sleep, feeling so grateful that they had both made it through the day alive.

For once he was almost sorry he didn't have a long drive home. "We're here," he said, gently jostling Liam's arm. Liam startled, waking up with wide, frightened eyes until he realized where he was.

"Sorry," Russ said, angry at himself for scaring Liam.

Liam shook his head as if trying to clear the sleep from his eyes. "Don't be. No matter how you woke me today, you'd probably get the same response."

Russ went around to help Liam down, and this time, his boyfriend's pride didn't keep him from accepting a hand. "Just so you know," Russ said, "Drew invited Noah to stay with us for a few days while he gets his wits about him."

"Noah?" Liam's brows furrowed.

"The Canadian Lynx? Turns out he actually is Canadian. Anyhow, Drew got assigned to help him when we left the shack, and Ty got to be the handler for the ocelot. Haven't met him yet."

Russ let them into the house and got their coats hung up in the front hall before leading Liam into the living room to settle on the couch, snuggled up against each other.

"The Huntsman put us in cages where we couldn't have fit, even if we were able to shift," Liam said, so quietly Russ almost missed it. "I think the lynx had given up."

"He'd been there the longest," Russ replied, tamping down his anger at the Huntsman, which served no purpose right now.

"The Huntsman had gone to get his truck and his ATV," Liam continued, almost as if he hadn't heard. "He planned to cart the cages down on the ATV, load everything into his hauler, and we'd be gone to Montana before anyone knew."

Montana. He'd have vanished, and we would never have known what happened.

Liam looked up at Russ and put a hand over his heart. "I can feel your fear in my mind."

"It's the mate bond. It gets stronger with time."

"And you're reading me?"

Russ nodded. "Aftershocks. Tiredness. Guilt, like you didn't do enough when you totally did," he added with a pointed look.

"Whatever he did to ward the cabin, I couldn't pick up anything from outside," Liam said. "I tried to send a message through the bond, even though I was far away, but I couldn't. And then when you came, I couldn't sense you. I wasn't even sure the key-finder would work."

"That was clever," Russ said, reaching over to push a lock of Liam's hair out of his eyes. "My cunning fox."

He leaned in to capture Liam's mouth, gently at first, then with more fervor. He'd always seen people on TV who followed up on nearly dying with a frantic round of sweaty sex. Now that his adrenaline rush had crashed, Russ was far more in the mood for slow, lingering, cherishing sex, the kind that said "I love you" and "I almost lost you" and "I treasure you" with every move.

Liam turned toward him to deepen the kiss, and brought one hand up to tangle in Russ's dark hair. Russ licked at Liam's lips, and Liam opened to him.

A car pulled into the driveway. Russ ignored it, figuring Drew could pretend he didn't see them. Then someone knocked at the door, and Russ drew back from Liam reluctantly.

"Either Drew forgot his keys, or we have a visitor. Don't forget where we left off," Russ added with a wink.

The cabin wasn't on the way to anywhere, so few people ever just "stopped in." Russ glanced out the window, wary. He relaxed when he saw the sheriff's SUV in the driveway.

"It's Armel," he called to Liam as he opened the door.

"Hi, Russ. Is Liam with you?" Torben Armel asked. His big frame filled the doorway.

"I just brought him back from the hospital," Russ said. "What do you need?" His wolf bristled, ready to protect against any intrusion.

"I just thought you might want to know what we found after you left," Armel replied.

"Come on in," Russ stood aside, resigned to the interruption.

"Good to see you up and around," Armel said with a nod to Liam. Russ sat on the couch beside his boyfriend, and Armel eyed the armchairs, then must have decided they might not hold his bulk, since he remained standing.

Liam just nodded, and Russ sensed the tension ratcheting back up in his mate. He slipped an arm around Liam's shoulder for support.

"It's been a long day, Sheriff," Russ said. "We're both pretty beat. I'm afraid we're not going to be much for small talk."

Armel nodded. "Let me cut to the chase. We found the kidnapper's truck and hauler, down on the old access road. According to the wallet in the truck, his name is Jerome Campbell. Sound familiar?"

Both Russ and Liam shook their heads. "Never heard of him," Russ said, and Liam echoed his comment.

"I didn't figure you had, but I needed to ask. I've put the word out to shifter law enforcement to see if we can link him to other disappearances. But we did find a logbook. Looks like he didn't trust computers or the internet. We need to go over it thoroughly, but I think there's enough material to make a convincing case to the Tribunal," the sheriff said.

"Good to hear," Russ replied.

"We also found something surprising when we looked at his phone," Armel went on. "There were several calls to a local number. Turns out, he and Eric Roberts are acquainted."

Russ couldn't place the name, but Liam sat up straight. "From the Fox Institute? The Scholar-in-Residence?" He turned to Russ. "He's the one who fought with Dr. Jeffries about hiring me because he wanted the job for his nephew."

"We picked up Roberts for questioning," Armel said. "Turns out that the Institute isn't a fan of his, now that they've seen him up close. There's apparently some concern that he overstated—or falsified—his credentials, including any ability as a 'psychic.' And there's a plagiarism claim against his books. But here's another interesting 'coincidence'…were you aware he taught at Cornell?"

Liam's eyes widened. "Shit. Kelson—my ex, the one who hired the Huntsman—went to Cornell for his undergraduate degree. I met Kelson while I was doing graduate work at Ithaca."

Armel nodded. "Uh-huh. Was your ex a shifter?"

Liam shook his head. "No. I don't think he knew anything about us until I confided in him…when I thought we were serious about each other," he added, chagrined. Russ kissed his temple, silently supporting him. Liam squeezed his hand, but Russ didn't need their bond to see the regret and self-recrimination that Liam harbored.

We're going to need to talk about this…later.

"So it would be very unlikely that Kelson, who knew nothing about shifters, would know how to hire a legendary hitman most of our community thought was a myth, don't you think?" Armel mused aloud. "That would be something that a person steeped in supernatural lore might know, though."

"You think Roberts connected Kelson to the Huntsman," Russ said in a flat, cold voice.

"Campbell—the Huntsman—knew Roberts well enough to have had a couple of phone conversations with him. As much as Roberts wanted his nephew to have the library job, I doubt he would have hired the Huntsman to get rid of you. But he might have put him in touch with an ex-student who needed a favor," Armel theorized, "especially if doing so helped him out too."

"Shit," Russ muttered. That was the loose end he hadn't been able to tie up in his mind, how someone had put the Huntsman on Liam's trail to begin with. In the end, it turned out to be a simple case of old school ties.

"So what? You think Kelson, for some reason, reached out to his old professor for advice about how to kill a shifter because he knew the professor claimed to be a psychic?" Liam asked in a quiet voice. He had paled, and Russ felt the tremors running through his lover's body.

"Something like that," Armel said with a shrug. "We're still working out the details. Dr. Jeffries has rallied the folks at the Institute to provide their full cooperation. Which is likely to include taking part in Campbell's questioning."

"Even if you can tie it back to Kelson, there's no way to charge him with anything, is there? Not without exposing the community," Liam nearly whispered. Russ could feel his fast, shallow breathing. He squeezed Liam's arm, a silent show of support.

"It's not so much about 'charging' him," Armel said, "as convincing him of the error of his ways. We have members of the community in his area who will be paying Kelson a visit to explain the consequences of his actions. We will make sure he doesn't try any do-overs. Not on my fuckin' watch." His low growl was all bear.

"Thank you," Liam said in a ragged voice. He sagged against Russ, who picked up a mix of relief and exhaustion through their bond.

Armel's expression softened as he looked at the two of them. "I'm sorry this has been your welcome to Fox Hollow. Russ can tell you; this isn't normal around here. I hope it doesn't change your mind about staying. Town like this needs a good head librarian."

Liam smiled and took Russ's hand, turning to meet his boyfriend's gaze. "I'm definitely staying," he said, and Russ's heart soared. "With my mate."

Armel smiled at that. "Good to know. I've got to get going, but I'll keep you informed."

Russ walked him to the door. "Thank you," he said. "For everything."

Armel smirked. "Thought you'd want to know that the Institute has decided to reach out to more witches, after the way the Huntsman used wardings to shut out the psychics. Dr. Jeffries said he knows people in Myrtle Beach and Cape May who agreed to recommend some people, and he plans to draw in the folks like that we already have in the area. So Fox Hollow is about to add a little more to its 'diversity.'"

"It's about time," Russ replied. "Stay in touch."

He closed the door and locked it, then went back to where Liam waited on the couch. Russ sat and opened his arms, and Liam came to him, wrapping his arms around Russ and kissing him like a drowning man.

"I need you," Liam breathed between desperate kisses. "I want this. Now."

"Your back...your tail..."

"I'll be fine. Good drugs, remember? I love you, Russ. I know it's fast, and it's crazy, but we're fated mates, and I don't ever want to regret not having every minute I can with you, as much as you'll give me."

Russ didn't try to hide his growl. He swept Liam up in his arms and carried him to the bedroom. "Let's get a bath, get the blood and sweat off both of us. Maybe give you that massage. And then, if you're still in the mood, I'll do anything you want me to do."

11

LIAM

NORMALLY, LIAM'S PRIDE WOULD HAVE REQUIRED RESISTING BEING swooped into a bridal carry, even by his big, strong, sexy wolf. Not tonight. He had worn out the badass side of himself fighting the Huntsman and needed a chance to rest and recharge. And although Russ had put up a good front, Liam knew his boyfriend also hadn't completely healed.

Maybe we can take care of each other, he thought.

"Just stretch out and relax. I'll run the bath," Russ said, setting Liam down gently on his king-size bed.

Liam gave a tentative stretch and winced when his back twinged. He rolled on the comforter, taking in Russ's scent, leaving behind his own. Liam heard the water running, and before long, Russ reappeared, already naked.

"Let's get you out of those clothes and into the tub," Russ said and sat on the edge of the bed to help. "Once the water loosens you up, I can try massaging your back. And go from there."

He wiggled his eyebrows mock-suggestively, but Liam knew Russ would hold off on making love if Liam didn't feel up to it.

Liam had no intention of backing off now.

Russ stuck close but let Liam make it to the bathroom on his own. He walked into the steamy room and paused to look at the big tub.

"Wow. You weren't kidding." When he had been at Russ's house before, the curtain had been drawn, so Liam hadn't noticed the jacuzzi that was definitely big enough for two.

"We put in the biggest one they had when we remodeled, since if you hadn't noticed, Drew and I aren't exactly small," Russ said. He nodded toward a door on the other side of the spacious bathroom. "Since it was too expensive and difficult to do two tubs, we decided to just make it a shared bathroom, first come, first bathed."

Liam sniffed the air, picking up a fresh, clean scent he couldn't quite place. "What do I smell?"

"Epsom salts," Russ replied. "I've come home from a lot of fires with pulled muscles. Ty's mother recommended them. It helps with soreness, and uh, it makes the water feel nice," he added, cheeks coloring a bit.

"Sounds wonderful." Liam wasn't about to tease his wolf for some necessary pampering.

Russ got into the tub first, then settled down and spread his legs. "I think we'll fit better like this. Come on in. The water's just right."

Liam felt a little shy as he climbed in and then nestled against Russ. The water was just hot enough to be soothing without scalding his balls, a delicate balance. He scooted back and felt his ass grind against Russ's half-hard cock.

"Just relax," Russ coaxed. He dipped his hands in the water, then brought them up, warm and slick, to gently work the knots out of Liam's shoulders. Liam leaned into Russ's hands, closing his eyes and enjoying the connection.

"Have you ever gotten a massage?" Russ asked, never losing his rhythm.

Liam moaned in response. The pressure hurt, but in the best sort of way, and Russ hadn't even gotten to his sore back.

"Always wanted to. Didn't have the money. You...do that really well."

"I messed up my back at the garage trying to lift something that was too heavy," Russ replied as he worked his way over Liam's shoulder blades. Liam wriggled a little from side to side when the pressure got intense.

"I froze up. Almost couldn't move," Russ went on. "They gave me some pain meds and a muscle relaxant, but that didn't work, so they sent me for physical therapy. Some of which turned out to be massage. Got me out of pain and back on my feet pretty fast. Been a believer ever since."

Liam tried to pay attention, but the combination of the hot water and Russ's hands put him in a state of utter bliss.

Mate. Must have our mate, his fox demanded.

Wait your turn.

"Now let's get your hair clean," Russ said. Liam ducked down and came up completely soaked. Russ did the same a moment later. They took turns working the aromatic herbal shampoo through each other's hair, massaging the scalp beneath, and then sank into the water to rinse away the soap.

Liam shimmied his ass against Russ's hard cock. His own had firmed up, getting on board with the program. "That feels good...but having you fuck me would feel better."

"Mmmm," Russ growled against Liam's ear. "Too hard on your back. How about you fuck me?"

Liam almost turned all the way around at that. He had wondered whether Russ would insist on topping. Liam didn't mind being a bottom, but he preferred to switch. "You'd do that?"

Russ stroked Liam's hair and his face. "Of course. No matter how we do it, it's gonna be good."

Russ gently turned Liam so that their positions were reversed, and Russ straddled his lap. He slid a hand between them, wrapping it around both their stiff cocks, giving them both a few tugs.

"Don't want to come like that," Liam groaned. "Want to be in you."

"Then let's finish here, and take this to the bedroom. Probably easier on your back anyhow." Russ helped him out of the deep tub and rubbed him down with a wonderfully big, thick bath sheet. Apparently wolves indulged in some of the finer things when it came to making a comfortable den.

The hot bath loosened Liam's muscles enough that he protested being scooped up again and insisted on walking to the bedroom to stretch a bit. They were both still naked, wonderfully warm, and smelling of the shampoo and soap Liam had come to associate with "pack" and "mate."

"Stretch out, face down, and I'll finish that massage," Russ cajoled. "That'll make sex more comfortable, too."

"I like any excuse for you to touch me," Liam practically purred, splaying himself across the bed.

Russ settled himself between Liam's legs. "Is this okay? I don't want to put any strain on your sore back."

"It's perfect. I like having you between my legs," Liam replied.

Russ worked his fingers down the tense muscles on either side of Liam's spine, and his strong thumbs dug into the spot at the base of Liam's backbone, where his tail anchored in shifter form.

Then his hands moved lower, thumbs digging into the outside of Liam's hips, fingers massaging his ass cheeks. Oddly enough, it didn't feel sexual, it just felt good.

"Did you know people hold tension in their hips?" Russ asked, moving back up to Liam's lower back.

"Uh-huh," Liam groaned. "Did you know that mind-blowing orgasms release tension?"

"Don't worry—I'm gonna be balls deep before this is over," Russ promised him. "How about I turn you over so you have support for your back—and you can watch me ride you."

"I like how you think," Liam snarked.

Russ slicked up his fingers with lube from a bottle on the night-stand and reached around to his hole, giving Liam a show as he opened himself up. Liam got his fingers slippery and then batted Russ's hand out of the way and ran the pad of his finger around his rim, teasing and stroking, then pressed two fingers inside, slowly, taking his time. Russ hissed with the stretch, but pressed into it, wanting more. Liam twisted his fingers just so, brushing across Russ's sweet spot.

"Keep doing that and it'll be over before we get started," Russ moaned, bucking against Liam's fingers to hurry him along.

"Getting you ready so we both enjoy it," Liam told him. He added a third finger and relished how tight Russ felt.

Everything seemed…more. His heart soared, his body felt like every cell was alive with need, and his fox yipped and whined for his mate.

"Let me do the work," Russ whispered. "Just enjoy the ride."

Liam withdrew his fingers and gripped Russ's hips with both hands, maneuvering him into position over his aching cock. "Take it slow," Liam urged. "We've got all night."

Liam looked up into Russ's face, memorizing his expression, seeing everything he needed in his mate's green eyes. Russ pushed down, and the head of Liam's cock sank into his tight heat, past the first ring of muscle and then deeper.

"Oh, my God. You feel so good," Liam groaned. Russ looked mighty fine too, as the muscles in his thighs and ass flexed, lifting him up and down, controlling his descent, and then sinking all the way to bottom out against Liam's balls.

"It's been a very long time," Russ said, rising and then impaling himself on Liam's long, elegant prick. "I haven't done this often."

Liam didn't want to discuss Russ's dead husband now that they were finally, finally, completing their bond. Then he realized that wasn't Russ's point. Whatever had been between Russ and Anthony, this was a part of himself Russ hadn't shared easily, an intimacy he was freely giving to Liam now, even when their relationship was still so new.

"Thank you," Liam said, meeting Russ's gaze. "For trusting me with this."

People in the shifter community made assumptions. Wolves were dominant. Foxes were twinks. Bears were…bears. Bobcats were jocks. And on and on. Defying those assumptions required courage and trust. Liam realized the gift he'd been given—to be accepted for his own badass self, and to see Russ being vulnerable.

Russ moved his hips in a figure eight, drawing a groan from Liam. He ran calloused fingers over Liam's sensitive nipples, making him shiver. Liam bucked up, then remembered his back was supposed to hurt. He felt a twinge, but the hot channel around his very sensitive cock cancelled out any discomfort.

"Does that feel good?" Liam asked and saw how his words turned Russ on.

"Really good," Russ groaned. "So perfect, my sexy fox."

Liam leaned forward and kissed Russ's chest, sucking on one pink nub and then the other until they pebbled beneath his tongue and lips. "My very sexy wolf," he breathed.

Russ ducked his head to capture Liam's mouth, thrusting with his tongue in time with the rhythm of his hips. The kiss turned from sweet to demanding quickly, and Liam reached between them to stroke Russ back to hardness and keep him stiff and ready. Liam loved the brush of Russ's scruff against his cheek and the scrape of his calloused hands as they skimmed his body, bringing him closer and closer to climax.

"Claim me," Russ breathed, nipping lightly at Liam's lips, not enough to draw blood but sufficient to gain his attention. "Come for me. Fill me up."

Russ growled and began moving in earnest, and Liam mirrored the pace with his hand, providing a slick channel for his lover's cock. Russ's green eyes were lust-blown, dilated so the black pupil had just a thin ring of green around it.

"Your eyes practically glow," Russ murmured.

Liam moved slightly, baring his neck. "I want your mark." One more stroke and Liam felt himself begin to tip over the edge. He tugged again at Russ's hard dick and felt hot come spill over his fist.

Russ dropped his mouth to the base of Liam's neck and bit down as his orgasm crashed through him, leaving a bite that would scar. Liam moaned at the bite and bucked his hips, wrapping one arm around Russ and drawing him close as he stroked his lover through the aftershocks.

"C'mon, Liam. Do it." Russ canted his head to one side, exposing his neck, begging for Liam to mark him.

As Liam felt his orgasm build, he closed his mouth over the spot where Russ's neck and shoulder met, and bit, breaking the skin and completing their bond.

Liam came harder than he could ever remember, and his vision nearly whited out for a moment. He licked over the teeth marks on Russ's shoulder, deep enough to scar but not damaging. The tang of blood brought his fox to the fore in his mind.

Finally. Took long enough. With that, his fox gave an imperious swish of his tail and receded, giving them privacy once more.

"I love you," Russ murmured. His arms bracketed Liam's head. Liam slid the flat of his tongue over the bite once more, and lifted his face for a gentle kiss, knowing Russ could taste his own blood on Liam's lips.

"Love you too," Liam replied, just loud enough to carry the few inches between them. "So, I guess this mate thing is official now, huh?"

Russ nuzzled Liam's ear, licking at the shell and gently sucking on the lobe, then kissing his way down to run his tongue over Liam's matching bite. The touch made Liam shiver, deep inside, and sent a twitch through his cock, which was still buried deep inside his lover.

"How's your back," Russ asked, raising a hand to touch Liam's cheek. Liam leaned into his palm, loving the feel of it against his skin.

"Better. All those good orgasm brain chemicals cancelled everything else," Liam replied, feeling sated and suddenly sleepy. He reluctantly, carefully, pulled out, immediately missing the hot clench of Russ's tight ass.

"Good," Russ said and kissed the top of Liam's head. "Let's clean up and get some sleep. It's been a long day."

"I don't have any clothes here," Liam remembered.

"I think I've got some that will fit, at least enough to get you home in the morning." Russ hesitated, and Liam felt a hint of worry through their bond. He dug around in his dresser, and came back with a pair of basketball shorts and a T-shirt. To Liam's surprise, they fit well enough that he didn't need to go back to his house in his fur to avoid scandalizing the neighbors.

When they had settled back into bed, Russ ran his fingers though Liam's soft hair, and Liam traced the outline of the rapidly healing bite on Russ's shoulder with his finger, still marveling at what had transpired between them.

"Hey, Liam," Russ said quietly, as they lay face-to-face beneath the covers, hands lightly tracing each other's bodies in a comfortable after-glow. "I know it's probably too soon, but I'd like you to consider moving in with me. When you're ready."

Liam gave him a sleepy smile. He'd had that thought and argued himself out of bringing it up just yet. "With Drew here and maybe Noah too?" He could tell Russ's little brother was crushing on the handsome lynx. From what Ty had mentioned to Russ at the hospital, Carlos the ocelot shifter planned to return to New York City.

Russ shrugged, never stopping the gentle roaming of his hands as if he were trying to memorize the contours of every inch of Liam's form. "The cabin has already been expanded. There's a good bit of elbow room, plus open land around us to run. The plot is big enough for a second cabin if it came to that."

He cleared his throat. "I'm not trying to pressure you or impose on your independence," he said, and Liam wondered if his mate had practiced beforehand, finding Russ's nervousness endearing. "But I hate sleeping apart from you. It drives my wolf crazy. He whines about going and sleeping on your porch to protect you. I've explained 'stalk-ing.' He doesn't get it."

"I don't like being away from you either," Liam replied quietly, running his finger lightly over Russ's cheekbones, around the curve of his ear, and then through his thick gray and brown hair.

"The bungalow is cute and comfortable," Liam went on, giving voice to what he had been thinking. "But it belongs to the library, so I can't change anything. And it's too small for the two of us. If I move in with you, it can become additional meeting space for small groups, and we could expand the library's community outreach."

Russ laughed. "My clever fox." He leaned forward to kiss the tip of Liam's nose. "Is that a yes?"

Liam took a moment to think, although he didn't have to go far for his fox's opinion, since it paced back and forth in his mind, tail swishing madly to get his human-half's attention. Under other circum-stances, this would be moving way too quickly. But they were fated mates, and their bond was sealed by consummation and the bites. A forever love. Soulmates. That changed everything.

"Yes," Liam replied. "Definitely a yes." He cupped his hand behind Russ's head and drew him close for a long, lingering kiss. Neither one of them had the energy for a second round tonight, but Liam didn't mind. He was more than content to curl up in his mate's arms, safe in the home they would soon share, right where he belonged.

12

LIAM

Six Months Later

"I THINK this is the best Fall Fling Fox Hollow has ever had," Russ said as he and Liam stood arm in arm watching the crowds go past on the sidewalk. "Which is due, in no small part, to a certain foxy librarian," he added, giving Liam a squeeze.

Liam leaned into him, basking in the praise. "I certainly didn't do it all by myself. Linda and Maddi played a huge role, and so did Dr. Jeffries. And all the volunteers. It took the whole town and the Institute to pull it off."

He could feel Russ shrug, even through their heavy coats. The short summer had ended, and the fall days already carried a nip in the air that promised snow. "The Fling has always been nice, but this year takes it to a whole new level. And you're the only thing that changed. So..."

Liam couldn't argue that the planning had taken a lot of time and effort—and all his fox and Leo charm to gather donors, volunteers, and enthusiasm behind several additions and enhancements.

The summer arts and theater program for kids, teens, and seniors led to a new gallery of artwork in the community center, as well as several new outdoor art installations that would rotate with the seasons. The Saranac Theater offered a screening of short films by local student filmmakers and a play produced and directed by participants in the program.

Once Eric Roberts's embarrassing lectureship abruptly ended, the Institute not only helped raise funds for the new summer and fall initiatives, but ramped up their slate of guest speakers, special community classes, psychic and tarot readings, drum circles, and more to surpass anything from prior years.

The result was a busy week for the town's shops, restaurants, and lodging, a last-hurrah before the snow fell, and things got quiet. As Russ and Liam meandered under the strings of twinkle lights and past the artwork that adorned the windows of every shop in town, it felt like everyone stopped to say hello to one or both of them.

I have my mate. I'm home.

"Come on. We don't want to miss the fireworks." Liam tugged Russ toward the beach, where a crowd had started to gather. Some of Russ's friends from the fire station were on a barge out on the water, ready to set off an array of explosives likely to rival the display on the Fourth of July.

"By the way, we have the cabin to ourselves tonight," Russ mentioned off-handedly. "Everybody's going to be at an all night gaming marathon at Brandon's."

Despite the cold, the Fox Hollow Big Brass Band struck up a rousing Sousa march. A flame appeared in the dark out on the water. Minutes later, the spectacle began as bright hues and glittering gold and silver lit up the night. The crowd clapped and cheered as each round out-did its predecessor, leading up to a grand finale that filled the sky with color and light that made Liam catch his breath.

He was so focused on the display that he hadn't noticed Russ's movement until he felt a tug at the hem of his parka. Russ knelt in front of him, holding out a small black box. People in the crowd began to nudge one another, turning to watch.

"Liam Reynard, my love, my fated mate. Will you do me the honor of also being my husband?" Russ asked, tears shining in his eyes, just like the tears that made their way, despite the cold, down Liam's face.

"Yes! Of course. Oh, God. Yes!"

The crowd cheered again, this time helping Liam and Russ celebrate as Liam pulled Russ to his feet and yanked him by the collar into a heated kiss.

"Do you want your ring?" Russ asked when they finally broke apart.

"In the sand, in the dark? Are you kidding?" Liam replied. "You can put it on my finger when we get home, where the light's nice and bright, and I can get a good look at it." He didn't mention that he'd had a ring stashed away for Russ for months, waiting for the right time. The thought of surprising Russ with his ring made Liam's smile even broader.

Liam couldn't wait to get back to the cabin that had come to feel like home. Well-wishers stopped them every few feet as the news spread, and while Liam appreciated their words of congratulations, he also despaired of ever making it back to the auto shop where Russ had parked.

The crowd from the fireworks had nearly dispersed as Russ eased out of the garage's lot, mindful of pedestrians that seemed determined to dart in front of his truck. Now that the big surprise was over, Russ looked nervous in the dim glow of the dashboard lights.

"I hope you'll like the ring," he fretted. "And if it doesn't fit right, or you want something else, we can take it back."

"It will be fine. I'm sure I'll love it," Liam assured him. "And I love you, too."

"Love you right back," Russ replied with a grin. "Were you surprised?"

"Mostly." Liam didn't know what Russ had been planning, but his fox's whiskers had been twitching all week with the sense that something was in the offing. "I thought you were up to something good, but I didn't know what."

"Hard to keep a secret with a mate bond."

"Hardly any I'd want to keep." At first, he'd been wary of strengthening his connection to Russ out of the fear that it would feel invasive, like having someone go through the things in his room without permission.

But the reality was entirely different. Without walls between them, he and Russ had learned to navigate soft boundaries, while avoiding stupid fights over misunderstandings or insecurities. For the first time in his life, Liam felt loved for all of who he was, and he loved Russ in the same way.

Nothing could ever be better.

When they got back to the cabin, Russ didn't waste any time after they stripped off coats and boots. He sank down on one knee in the kitchen beneath the glare of the fluorescent overhead light, and presented the box to Liam once more. This time, he opened the lid, showing off a beautiful rose gold band.

"Yes," Liam breathed, answering the unasked question. Russ slid the ring on the third finger of Liam's right hand, a promise and a statement until their wedding day when the ring would move to the left hand during the ceremony.

"It's beautiful," he said, holding his hand out so the light reflected from the gold, making it shine.

"It looks even better on you." Russ rose to his feet and pulled Liam in for a tender kiss.

Liam surprised him by giving him a peck and then twisting out of his arms. "Wait there."

He hurried to the bedroom and tore through his underwear drawer, cursing under his breath until he found the elusive box, hidden inside a sock. Liam sent the sock flying and rushed back to where Russ still stood in the kitchen with a look of utter confusion on his face.

Liam dropped to his knees before he even stopped moving like he was a batter sliding into third base. He came to a halt at Russ's feet and held up his offering in both hands with a nervous smile.

"I, um, might have been thinking along the same lines," he said, as Russ stared at the ring box with wide eyes. "Just wasn't sure when the time would be right."

When Russ didn't move and didn't say anything, Liam's anxiety rose. His tongue flicked over his lips nervously. "Ah...Russ?"

That snapped Russ out of his daze, and he cupped both of his larger hands around Liam's, with the ring box in the center. "How long?" he managed in a voice tight with emotions.

Liam shrugged, a little embarrassed. "About a month after I moved in," he admitted. "I mean, it seemed like a no-brainer after the whole mate bond thing. I don't care what kind of ceremony. Whatever you want. Do wolves do something special? Does Fox Hollow even have a Justice of the Peace?"

He knew he was babbling, wondering what was taking Russ so long to just open the damn box. Russ grinned at him fondly and placed a finger to Liam's lips to stop the nervous torrent of words. Liam promptly sucked Russ's finger into his mouth with an obscene slurp and began to give it a good approximation of an enthusiastic blow job which had the desired effect, judging from the growing bulge in Russ's jeans.

"I was afraid that you might not be ready yet," Russ admitted. "I thought you might turn me down. So I was just surprised you bought me a ring first."

"Turn you down? Never. And the whole fated mates connection helped a lot with being ready," Liam replied. "So whaddya say, Wolfie? Gonna make an honest fox out of me?" He knew Russ read his wise-cracking for the defense mechanism it was.

Russ's hands shook as he reached for the box and opened the lid. He stared, dumbfounded, at a ring that was a perfect duplicate of the one he had presented to Liam, only sized larger, and then looked at his mate with puzzled astonishment. "How?"

Liam smiled through his tears, too overwhelmed by emotion to try to hide his feelings. "I don't know. But when I saw it, I knew it was the right one. I even went all the way up to Saranac Lake to get it so you wouldn't know."

Russ managed a wet chuckle, as his own eyes filled. "I went down to Lake George for the same reason."

"May I?" Liam asked, totally serious now. Russ nodded, swallowing hard.

"Russ Lowe, heart of my heart, peanut butter to my jelly, my perfect match—will you marry me?"

"Yes. Yes. Yes." Instead of pulling Liam up, Russ sank to his knees to join him, letting Liam slide the ring onto his finger. They reached for each other at the same time, coming together in a fierce kiss. Tongues, lips, and hands claimed and explored as clothing went flying.

"Forever," Russ growled, lying atop Liam on the floor once they had both gotten completely naked.

Liam flipped them so that he straddled Russ, looking down with an insolent grin. "Always," he answered, grabbing for the lube they kept in a corner of the junk drawer.

Which is how they woke up the next morning, sated, chilly, and stuck together, entwined on the kitchen floor after a marathon session that pushed the boundaries of even shifter stamina.

"Damn," Russ said, brushing the hair out of Liam's eyes. "We should get engaged more often. Although I'm not sure I can walk, between my back and my ass."

Liam kissed him, unconcerned about morning breath. "I think you wore out my dick." He threw one leg over Russ's muscular thigh and started to grind against it, loving the scrape of wiry body hair against his most sensitive skin. "Nope. My bad. Looks like it's working just fine," he smirked, knowing Russ could feel his erection growing between them.

Russ got to his feet and scooped Liam into his arms in one move. "First, a shower." He wrinkled his nose. "I'm crusty."

Liam gave him a lascivious grin. "Whose fault is that?"

Russ rolled his eyes. "Then, we brush teeth. My mouth tastes like balls. *Your* balls, to be specific."

"Didn't hear any complaints last night," Liam snarked, lazily kicking his legs up and down from the knees like something out of a 1950s romcom.

"And before we do anything else with my cock, I seriously need to take a leak."

Liam arched backward, flinging his arms out in mock surrender, knowing Russ wouldn't let him fall. "*Fine*," he said in mock dismay, letting his fox do its diva best. "Interrupt our epic lovemaking. I only hope we can somehow regain our momentum."

"Oh, I have plenty of *momentum* for you," Russ replied, bucking his hips to jab Liam in the ass with his rapidly filling cock. "After we clean up." He leaned down to nuzzle Liam's ear. "I can't wait to get you all dirty again."

Liam booped him on the nose. "Challenge accepted."

AFTERWORD

I grew up going camping in the Adirondacks, and those mountains have always held a special corner of my heart. I love the smell of the pine trees, the contours of the land, the beauty of the lakes. After not having been back for a long time, I went for a visit a few years ago and found that not much had changed, and it was just as special as I remembered.

The town of Fox Hollow is very loosely based on Long Lake, which was the closest town to where we tent-camped. There is a Victorian hotel there (great food, cool interior), seaplane rides, an awesome gift shop, and a terrific ice cream place, in case you're in the neighborhood. Everything else is totally my imagination.

The Saranac Theater's decor was inspired by an independent theater in Lake Placid. Liam's attempt to talk with the non-shifter foxes was based on my effort to use my long-ago college Spanish to communicate in Barcelona a few years ago. I got the point across, but inelegantly, with weird conjugation. But we still communicated, which was the goal.

The "forever wild" Adirondacks are a dangerous place. People do go missing. One particular incident that happened when I was a kid has never been solved. You're likely to encounter bear and other wild animals, and the terrain is vast and unforgiving—but beautiful.

As for the Fox Institute, I've always been fascinated by the Spiritualist Movement and Lily Dale and all of the interest in psychics and mediums during the late 1800s. The Fox Sisters were real and were very famous before one of the sisters claimed everything had been faked. She later recanted, but it was too late. Some believe that their gift was real, but the pressure of becoming touring performers pushed them to go beyond what they could actually do. Lily Dale is an actual place, and it figured prominently in the Spiritualist Movement. The idea of supporters of the Fox Sisters being exiled is entirely fictional, but Fox Sisters and fox shifters seemed to go together in my mind!

All of my Morgan Brice series cross over with each other and with my urban fantasy stories written under my Gail Z. Martin name. So that mention of "knowing a guy" in Cape May and Myrtle Beach is a hint that you'll be seeing familiar faces pop up in future Fox Hollow books and vice versa!

Please also look for a related short story about a squirrel shifter looking for love in the Heart2Heart4 anthology and later, on Prolific Works. You'll also find another related story in the Beyond the Realm: Imagine linked series, and yet another in a "friend's-to-lovers" giveaway and ultimately on Prolific Works. Enjoy!

ALSO BY MORGAN BRICE.

Badlands Series

Badlands

Restless Nights, a Badlands Short Story

Lucky Town, a Badlands Novella

The Rising

Cover Me, a Badlands Short Story

Loose Ends

Leap of Faith, A Badlands/Witchbane Novella

Night, a Badlands Short Story

Fox Hollow Zodiac Series

Huntsman

Kings of the Mountain Series

Kings of the Mountain

Treasure Trail Series

Treasure Trail

Witchbane Series

Witchbane

Burn, a Witchbane Novella

Dark Rivers

Flame and Ash

Unholy

Badlands

Medium and clairvoyant Simon Kincaide owns a Myrtle Beach boardwalk shop where he runs ghost tours, holds séances, and offers private psychic readings, making a fresh start after his abilities cost him his lover and his job as a folklore professor. Jaded cop Vic D'Amato saw something supernatural he couldn't explain during a shootout several years ago in Pittsburgh and relocated to Myrtle Beach to leave the past behind, still skeptical about the paranormal. But when the search for a serial killer hits a dead end, Vic battles his skepticism to ask Simon for help. As the body count rises, Simon's involvement makes him a target, and a suspect. But Simon can't say no, even if it costs him his life and heart.

Read the first chapter free at MorganBrice.com

Kings of the Mountain

Fast cars. Outlaw country boys. Snarky werewolves, vengeful ghosts, menacing monsters, and a love that can't be denied.

Dawson King's family has been hunting things that go bump in the night in Transylvania County, North Carolina, since before the Revolutionary War.

Dawson was never happier than when he was racing his souped-up Mustang along winding mountain roads and hunting monsters with his best friend, Grady. Then Grady fell in love with him, which should have been perfect since Dawson had already fallen hard for Grady.

But Grady was only seventeen, and Dawson feared that sooner or later, Grady would realize his feelings were just a first crush, and then he'd be gone, leaving Dawson devastated. They both needed space to figure things out. So Dawson joined the army, while Grady stayed on the mountain.

Four years later, Dawson is coming home. He's more sure than ever Grady is his forever love, and they've both agreed to begin this new aspect of their relationship as soon as Dawson gets back.

Then Grady's father is killed in a werewolf hunt gone wrong. Grady is devastated, and he's throwing mixed signals about moving forward. Dawson knows he needs to hold off on this new thing between them until Grady has time to grieve. But monsters never sleep, and one hunt after another throws Dawson and Grady into constant danger, while tension and unresolved feelings ripple between them.

Making it even harder, Dawson's got a secret. He's dreamed of death omens—which point to something stalking Grady. Can Dawson figure out who's trying to kill Grady, save his life, and win back his heart?

Read the first chapter free at MorganBrice.com

Treasure Trail

Erik Mitchell traveled the world uncovering art fraud and relic theft, which pitted him against spoiled billionaires, unscrupulous collectors, mobsters, and cartels. He worked with law enforcement across the U.S. and Europe, but then a sting goes wrong, Erik ends up injured and returns to find his partner cheating. He decides to stop globetrotting and buy an antique shop in scenic Cape May, NJ, rebuild his life, and nurse his broken heart.

Undercover Newark cop Ben Nolan went down in a hail of bullets when a bust went sideways, after a tip-off from a traitor inside the department. When he recovers, he spends a couple of years as a private investigator, only to tire of seeing the worst of human nature. So when his aunt offers him the chance to take over her rental real estate business in Cape May, it seems too good to be true. Now if he could just believe he could ever be lucky again in love.

Sparks fly when Erik and Ben meet. But when a cursed hotel's long-ago scandals resurface, the two men are pulled into a web of lies, danger, and deception that will test their bond—and might make them Cape May's newest ghosts!

Read the first chapter free at MorganBrice.com

Witchbane

Seth Tanner and his brother Jesse's fun evening debunking local urban legends ends with Jesse's gruesome murder. Seth vows revenge on Jesse's killer - too bad the murderer has been dead for a hundred years. Seth uncovers a cycle of ritual killings that feed the power of a dark warlock's immortal witch-disciples, and he's hell bent on stopping Jackson Malone from becoming the next victim. He's used to risking his neck. He never intended to risk his heart.

Read the first chapter free at Morgan Brice.com

ACKNOWLEDGMENTS

It takes a village to get a book out into the world. As always, I want to thank my husband, Larry N. Martin, for all his behind-the-scenes work with brainstorming, editing, formatting, tracking, uploading, and so many other things that go into this crazy business of writing. Of course, there's also our editor, Jean Rabe, our cover artists, Adrijus Guscia and Melissa Gilbert, and the wonderfully supportive readers in my Worlds of Morgan Brice group and my Shadow Alliance group, as well as the Spookies in Reading Past The Realm. A huge "I luv you" goes out to all my readers everywhere! Because you read, I write.

I can't say "thank you" enough to my wonderful beta and ARC readers, including: Amy, Andy, Anne, Barbara, Beth, Beth, Bichter, Carol, Carra, Cheryl, Chris, Cindy, Collyn, Darrell, Debbie, Elayne, Eleanor, George, Grace, Jamie, Janel, Janet, Jeanne, Jenn, Judy, Karolina, Kendra, Laurie, Lexi, Lisa, Lydia Manuela, Mary, Mindy, Patti, Pavel, Perian, Rosalind, Sandra, Stacy, Susan, Susana, Suzanne, Tammi, and Xochtil.

ABOUT THE AUTHOR

Morgan Brice is the romance pen name of bestselling author Gail Z. Martin. Morgan writes urban fantasy male/male paranormal romance, with plenty of action, adventure, and supernatural thrills to go with the happily ever after.

Gail writes epic fantasy and urban fantasy, and together with co-author hubby Larry N. Martin, steampunk and comedic horror, all of which have less romance and more explosions.

On the rare occasions Morgan isn't writing, she's either reading, cooking, or spoiling two very pampered dogs.

Watch for additional new series from Morgan Brice, and more books in all of her universes coming soon!

Where to find me, and how to stay in touch

Join my Worlds of Morgan Brice Facebook Group and get in on all the behind-the-scenes fun! My free reader group is the first to see cover reveals, learn tidbits about works-in-progress, have fun with exclusive contests and giveaways, find out about in-person get-togethers, and more! It's also where I find my beta readers, ARC readers and launch team! Come join the party! www.Facebook.com/groups/WorldsOf-MorganBrice

Find me on the web at https://morganbrice.com. Sign up for my newsletter and never miss a new release! http://eepurl.com/dy_8oL. You can also find me on Twitter: @MorganBriceBook, on Pinterest (for Morgan and Gail): pinterest.com/Gzmartin, on Instagram as Morgan-BriceAuthor, and on Bookbub https://www.bookbub.com/authors/morgan-brice

Enjoy two free short stories set in my Badlands series. Read *Cover*

Me here for free: https://claims.prolificworks.com/free/iwZDEP9Z and *Restless Nights* here: https://claims.prolificworks.com/free/js6x0fq8

Come check out the ongoing, online convention ConTinual www.facebook.com/groups/ConTinual

Support Indie Authors

When you support independent authors, you help influence what kind of books you'll see more of and what types of stories will be available, because the authors themselves decide which books to write, not a big publishing conglomerate. Independent authors are local creators, supporting their families with the books they produce. Thank you for supporting independent authors and small press fiction!

Made in United States
Orlando, FL
04 November 2021

10204822R00111